MIDN1GHT FEAST

MIDN1GHT FEAST

Great stories for a great cause!

HarperCollins *Children's Books*

First published in paperback in Great Britain by HarperCollins *Children's Books* 2007
HarperCollins *Children's Books* is a division of HarperCollins*Publishers* Ltd
77-85 Fulham Palace Road, Hammersmith, London W6 8JB

The HarperCollins *Children's Books* website address is
www.harpercollinschildrensbooks.co.uk

War Child and No Strings are on the web at
www.warchild.org.uk
www.nostrings.ie

1

Acknowledgements

No Strings and War Child would like to thank the following people:

The contributors, who have all generously donated their time and talent.

Nick Lake, the editor for this edition, and Gillie Russell, the publisher for both this and *Kids' Night In*. Michelle Madden and Laura Harris at Puffin Books Australia, who edited and published the original edition in which several of these stories appeared, and the team of volunteer editors who helped them – Jessica Adams, Helen Basini, Nick Earls and Juliet Partridge.

Thanks also to Aschiana Street Children's Project, Sara Foster, Jonathan Lloyd, Johnie McGlade, OMAR, Ash Sweeting, Rosie Waller and Tara Wynne. For more information on this series of anthologies, and the money raised, please visit www.girlsnightin.info

Contents

Introduction by Fearne Cotton

Thank you so much for buying this shiny new copy of *Midnight Feast*! You have now officially done two Good Things.

Good Thing number 1: by buying this book, you have just given one pound to War Child and No Strings, who work all around the world to help children in countries devastated by war and poverty. Every purchase of *Midnight Feast* makes a real difference to suffering children.

Good Thing number 2: you have also got your hands on a brilliant, bumper collection of new stories by the world's most fabulous children's writers and illustrators, which will keep boredom at bay for many a day to come. All of these wonderful people have given their work *absolutely free*. We hope you enjoy it as much as we do!

So grab your favourite snacks, pull the covers over your head and turn on your torch: these stories are guaranteed to give you a warm feeling inside.

Fearne x

PSYCHIC CATS AND SPOOKY DOGS

Jessica Adams

Illustrated by Oliver Jeffers

Have you ever suspected that your dog might be psychic? Here's one way to find out. The next time everyone leaves the house for the day, set up a video camera on a tripod near the front door. If your pooch has a strong sixth sense, he will start scratching, barking and running around in circles or putting his paws up on the window ledge ten to twenty minutes before you get home. You can't trick psychic

....and ACTION!

dogs, even if you come home unusually early or unusually late. If your pet really does have super powers, then he'll always know when you're coming home. Scientist Rupert Sheldrake has spent years studying dogs who know what their owners are up to – so if you're curious about the scientific reasons for your pooch's behaviour, visit www.sheldrake.org

What about cats? Professional psychics believe they are natural healers. Try it for yourself. The next time you are feeling sick in bed, send a message using ESP (extrasensory perception) to your cat. You can do this by sending a strong, silent thought, like: "Help, I've got a headache!" or "SOS! I've got a stomach-ache."

You'll be surprised how many times your cat comes up and sits on you – or beside you – and if your favourite animal really does have healing paws, you'll start to feel better in just a few minutes.

It works the other way too. When my ginger cat, Henry, was bitten by a snake once, he woke me up in the middle of the night so I could put my hands on his head and give him healing. Henry had been bitten by a king brown – one of the most poisonous snakes in Australia. His pupils were as big as five-cent pieces. He kept falling over whenever he tried to walk. And even his breathing sounded bad, as if the air was rattling in his ribs.

Henry put his paws on the end of my bed and stayed there

while I sent him healing vibes all night long. And the good news is, he recovered enough to walk into the vet's surgery the next day for a blood transfusion! You can try this healing hands method yourself, the next time you have a wonky dog, or a sick cat or an upside-down goldfish. You'll still need the vet – but the healing should help too. And you'll be amazed at how many times animals (even fish) seem to come up to you to ask for it!

Some professional psychics specialise in treating animals instead of humans. Their job is to try and talk to the animals using ESP, to find out what's really going on inside their heads. An American pet psychic once had a pig as a patient. The pig was refusing to eat, and its owner was worried that the animal would waste away altogether.

Enter the pet psychic. And guess what? Once she had used her ESP to listen to the pig for a few minutes, she discovered that the pig's owner was divorcing his wife – and the pig was very upset about it, as it liked both of them.

Once the owner realised that was why his favourite pig was refusing to eat, he made the pig a promise – even though his wife was moving out, she would still come and visit once a week, to say hello. The result? The pig's eating habits were soon back to normal.

Animals are extremely sensitive. Pigs have even worked out how to play computer games (in return for prize treats of m&ms) so don't make the mistake of thinking they're just dumb animals.

a computer - playing pig

Can a pig really "talk" to a human, though? Try communicating with animals yourself, and experiment with a variety of different creatures. For the best results, you need to find peace and quiet, and choose a time when the animal has been fed and is looking relaxed — but not asleep.

Begin by saying "hello" in your head, and then tell the animal that you are going to try and communicate with it, using ESP. It helps to pat or stroke the animal as you are talking or, if you are trying to chat to a horse or a bird, to put your face up to the fence or the cage.

pet telepathy

Ask the animal if it would like you to do anything, then listen. What are you hearing? Often, animals ask for more food, but sometimes they can surprise you by asking for something else. One pet psychic I know was chatting to a Siamese cat one day, when it told her that it wanted its old playmate (another Siamese) back again.

Animals can be quite surprised that you are prepared to psychically listen to them at first, so you might need to practise until you get a talking/listening rhythm going. After all, most cats and dogs are used to being talked at, or yelled at, but they hardly ever get a chance to talk back.

Can animals really predict the future? Scientists monitoring earthquakes in California have discovered that household pets — and wild creatures too — change their behaviour several days

a fortune - te ll ing   dog

before a quake. In the future, watching the psychic behaviour of animals like this could help save lives.

My cat, Henry, always knows when I'm going away. Even before I've packed my case, he creates havoc in the house – running up and down the kitchen, waking me up in the middle of the night, and hanging upside down on the flyscreen (his favourite way to annoy me!).

Watch your cat or dog carefully, a few days before you go on holiday. Do you think they're picking something up?

Psychic skills are survival skills. They help animals to find food, water, shelter, healing and safety. If cats and dogs had mobile phones and email it might be different, but for now they're stuck with ESP and predicting the future instead.

Henry on his mobile phone

Be very careful if you leave your cat, dog or bird with someone when you go away and the animal either tries to get away or looks extra unhappy. Their instincts are seldom wrong, and the person you have chosen to mind them may not be the right one!

At the same time, if your dog or cat loves someone to bits, the chances are that this person is kind, generous and — surprise, surprise — loves animals. Pets, in particular, have a knack of "finding" the person they know is best designed to look after them.

If you want to run another test on your cat's or dog's psychic skills, play Food Hide and Seek. The idea is to hide yourself somewhere in the house or garden with an unopened can of dog or cat food and a can opener.

We all know dogs and cats run into the kitchen at the sound of a can being opened, or at the faintest sniff of fish or meat in the air, but what if they have no clues at all and are forced to use their psychic skills instead?

Make sure you hide yourself in a place your cat or dog wouldn't normally look. Under the bed is good, or even in the attic.

Send a psychic signal, using ESP, telling your animal that if they find you, you will open the can and give them some of their favourite food. Then wait and see what happens.

Extremely psychic dogs and cats only take a few minutes before they will run towards your secret spot – or even sit down under it/beside it and refuse to move! This is fun for your pet, as well as you, and it will help to strengthen the psychic bond between you.

If your cat or dog is super psychic, you can also ask them to guess anything, from Oscar results to election results. For this test, you will need to rip out photographs of famous actors and actresses (or politicians, like John Howard or Kim Beazley) and spread them out on the floor. Then, ask your dog or cat to go straight to the winner.

Make sure you don't use photographs from a newspaper that's been used to wrap fish and chips, though, or your pet will probably try to eat the actors and politicians, instead of pointing to them.

If you think your pet needs an extra challenge, you can try more psychic tests with photographs of yourself and your friends. Ask questions like:

Which person has a red bike?

Which person was on the winning relay team at the sports carnival?

Which person has a brother called Noah?

And so on...

Finally, remember that there is a very good reason why cats, dogs, birds and fish have such a strong sixth sense. It's because they spend their whole lives watching us. And that often makes them more in tune with human beings than you might think. Try it yourself and put it to the test – is your cat or dog as psychic as Henry?

ASK ANNIE

Meg Cabot

Ask Annie your most complex interpersonal relationship questions. Go on, we dare you!

All letters to Annie are subject to publication in the *Clayton High School Register*...

Dear Annie,

Help! I'm in love with a boy I've never met. He lives 2,000 miles away and works in the entertainment business. Still, when I see him on the big screen, and gaze into his blue eyes, I know that we are soul mates. I already have a boyfriend who's nice enough, but I'd leave him in a second if I ever got a chance to meet my REAL love, Luke Striker. What should I do?

Crushed

PS: I know your real identity is supposed to be a secret, but aren't you [this section deleted by Register staff]? 11th grade, sits at the middle table in the caff everyday with Scott Bennet and those other people from the school paper?

Dear Crushed,

There is a fine line between celebrity worship and stalking, and you sound ready to cross it. Surrender the fantasy and start concentrating on what's important: finishing school and getting into college.

And try to appreciate that boyfriend of yours a little more.

Some of us aren't lucky enough to have a boyfriend at all, real OR imaginary.

Annie

PS: Confidential to Crushed: you know I can't reveal my true identity. How would I be able to give unbiased advice otherwise?

To: JennyG
Fr: DramaQueen

OMG, did you HEAR???? Luke Striker is HERE, at THIS school! Supposedly he's playing a jock in his next movie, so he's here to research the role, since you know he never went to a real high school, just had on-set tutors his whole life. You should have SEEN Geri Lynn's face when she found out. But she hasn't liked him half as long as I have. I've loved him since his days on *Heaven Help Us*. CAN YOU BELIEVE IT????

✉

To: DramaQueen
Fr: JennyG

That's horrible, Trina! Geri's got Scott to think about! She's totally taking her boyfriend for granted. Which isn't fair to those of us who've never been lucky enough to get a boyfriend in the first place.

✉

To: JennyG
Fr: DramaQueen

Oh, puhlease, Jen. You could totally get a boyfriend if you wanted one. I TOLD you Scott Bennet liked you. But you act so shy around him, he never got the hint, so he asked Geri out instead. And look where that got him! She's getting ready to dump him for LUKE STRIKER!

✉

To: DramaQueen
Fr: JennyG

She's WHAT????

✉

To: JennyG
Fr: DramaQueen

You haven't heard? She even wrote to Ask Annie about it
– TWICE!

✉

To: DramaQueen
Fr: JennyG
THAT was GERI? I mean ? she DID?

✉

To: JennyG
Fr: DramaQueen
Totally! Check it out:

It's me, Crushed. You're never going to believe this...unless you really are [this section deleted by Register staff] , in which case, you already know. LUKE STRIKER is here, at this very school, researching a part for his next movie role. It's like a dream come true!!!! I know you said to try to appreciate my boyfriend more. But it's LUKE STRIKER!!!! And my boyfriend is cute and all, but he's nowhere NEAR as cute as Luke. WHAT SHOULD I DO???

Crushed Again

✉

To: JennyG
Fr: DramaQueen

And look what Annie said back. Talk about harsh!

Dear Crushed Again,

Do you have any idea how many letters I've got this week that are EXACTLY like yours? Every girl in this school is getting ready to dump her boyfriend for Luke Striker.

But none of you is considering the fact that when Luke's finished researching his movie role, he's going back to Hollywood. And it's highly unlikely he's going to be taking you with him. So you're going to be dumping your boyfriend for nothing. Which will leave you without a date for the Spring Fling (which isn't that big a deal. Some of us don't exactly have dates, and we're still managing to survive).

Is that what you want?

Annie

✉
To: DramaQueen
Fr: JennyG

I don't think Annie was being harsh. She's right. Especially if that letter really WAS from Geri, and she was talking about Scott. Scott is way cuter than Luke Striker!

✉
To: JennyG
Fr: DramaQueen

Um, only YOU would think Scott Bennet is cuter than Luke Striker, Jen. I wonder who Annie really is. I overheard Geri saying she thinks it's YOU! As if YOU would ever have the guts to do something like that.

✉

To: DramaQueen
Fr: JennyG

Ha. Yeah. Funny.

✉

To: JennyG
Fr: DramaQueen

OMG! Did you see the letter to Annie today????

Dear Annie,

I feel stupid writing this letter to you. But I guess it's OK since you'll never know it's me. I mean, who I am. Anyway, it's about my girlfriend. Like everybody else in this stupid school, she's gone ga-ga over this Luke Striker guy. Don't even ask me why — she barely knows him. It's just because he's rich and played Lancelot in that movie last year.

Anyway, the thing is... I'm not so sure I even care. I mean, I used to be sure I loved her, but lately I've been having a hard time keeping my mind off someone else... this girl I eat lunch with every day. She's really smart and has the cutest smile. In fact, I'm kind of hoping my girlfriend WILL dump me for this Striker guy, so I can ask this other girl to the Spring Fling. The problem is, this other girl is kind of shy, and I can't tell whether or not she likes me. What should I do?

Feverish in Fifth Period

✉

To: JennyG
Fr: DramaQueen

That HAS to be from Scott Bennet! About Geri! It just HAS to be! And OMG, Jen, the girl ? the shy one with the cute smile who he eats lunch with – has to be YOU!!!!! I TOLD you he likes you. ARE YOU FREAKING????

✉

To: DramaQueen
Fr: JennyG

That letter isn't about me! I don't have a cute smile. Scott barely even knows I'm alive. He must mean someone else.

✉

To: JennyG
Fr: DramaQueen

Oh, right. It CAN'T be you.
What do you think Ask Annie replied????

✉

To: DramaQueen
Fr: JennyG

Well, I think I can take a pretty good guess...

Dear Feverish,

    If your girlfriend doesn't realise what a great guy you are, she totally doesn't deserve you.

And as for this other girl, just because she isn't throwing herself at you the way some girls in this school might be throwing themselves at a certain movie star doesn't mean she doesn't like you. Maybe she's just shy. You'll never know unless you ask!

Good luck.

Annie

✉

To: JennyG
Fr: DramaQueen

So has Scott asked you to the Spring Fling yet????

✉

To: DramaQueen
Fr: JennyG

No! I told you, I'm not the girl he meant in that letter. Or he'd have broken up with Geri by now. But really Trina, it's OK. I mean, I never expected that he—

Dear Annie,

   Just a note to let you know I hate you. You told my boyfriend to break up with me! Just because I happen to like Luke Striker better! Well, I have news for you: Luke and I are going to the Spring Fling together. How do you like that????

   Crushed No More

✉

To: JennyG
Fr: DramaQueen

OMG!!! THEY BROKE UP!!! NOW do you believe me????

✉

To: DramaQueen
Fr: JennyG

Trina, cut it out. Scott's not – oh, no.

✉

To: JennyG
Fr: DramaQueen

Oh, no WHAT???

✉

To: DramaQueen
Fr: JennyG

I just got an email from—

✉

To: JennyG
Fr: DramaQueen

FROM WHO???? DON'T LEAVE ME IN SUSPENSE!!!

✉

To: JennyG
Fr: ScottB

So I'm taking your advice.
Will you go to the dance with me?

✉

To: ScottB
Fr: JennyG
Wait a minute. YOU KNOW I'M ASK ANNIE???

✉

To: JennyG
Fr: ScottB

Why not? You knew it was me, didn't you?
So. Will you?

Confidential to Feverish,

Yes!
Annie

A POLISH CHRISTMAS

Eoin Colfer

Warsaw is an old city, but its bricks and mortar are new. The German army flattened it on their way home in 1945. Grandpa told little Lucja this many times each week. And every time he told the story, Lucja imagined a giant black boot stepping out of the sky, crushing the city's spires and bridges. Sometimes these imaginings made her giggle. It *was* funny, like a cartoon. Grandpa did not like it when she laughed at his story. Lucja didn't know why he got upset. It wasn't as if his stories were true.

"Warsaw is not a city of buildings," he would insist. "It is a city of people. We have been here longer."

Lucja lived in an apartment on Targowa Street with Grandpa

Feliks and Mama Agata. There were many other families in the building, and in these families there were at least twelve other five-year-old girls. There may have been more, but Lucja could only count to twelve. She had never tried to go beyond twelve; in fact, twelve was her record, and by the time she got that far, she was already bored.

Lucja bored easily, and this was why she was no good at queuing. For the first ten seconds she was fine, but then her curiosity would burst out of her like air from a punctured balloon.

"Why is that woman so fat?" she would ask.

Or, "His nose is red, Mama. Why is his nose so red?"

The most embarrassing had been directed at Missus Jazinka in the queue for sausage. "Is there a shortage of tissue, Mama? Is there? Because that woman is wiping her nose on her sleeve, then her sleeve on that boy's head."

Lucja's mother had abandoned the queue, and they ate vegetables for a few days.

"You queue like an American," shouted Grandpa. "Everything has to be now. This is not New York City, Lucja. Here we queue. Warsaw will teach you that."

"Your button is loose," said Lucja, pointing out what she saw. As she always did. "And anyway, last Christmas there was no carp, even when you queued. I remember that."

It was true. Grandpa had taken on the duty of obtaining the Christmas Eve fish personally. He put newspapers in his shoes, stood in line for six hours outside the fishmongers and came home without even the smell of fish on his hands.

"That only happened once, you impertinent child," said Grandpa. "And it will not happen again. Neither Germans nor Communists will keep me from a fish steak this Christmas Eve."

"What does a German look like?" asked Lucja.

"Like a Communist," said Grandpa crossly. "But with better boots."

There were ways to obtain things without the dreaded queue. The old ways. Barter. People had things and they would trade them. Strictly speaking these people were breaking party law, but Moscow was a long way away, and citizens had to live. All but the most fanatical soldiers ignored the old women nonchalantly wandering the streets of Warsaw, hefting large baskets seemingly filled with rags.

One such *baba z cielecina* or "veal lady" arrived at the Kopec back door on Saint Nicholas' Day, two weeks before Christmas. She plonked her basket on the table, drawing back the cloth. The basket was lined with plastic bags and brimming with cuts of beef and boar.

Grandpa was listening to Abba on his cassette recorder, acting casual.

"*Gin-do-bray*, Kopec. What can I do for you today. A nice bit of beef?"

"Fish is what I want. Carp actually."

The veal lady pulled up a chair. This was serious business.

"Mama mia," she sighed, helping herself to a glass of water. "Here I go again. Carp, Kopec? That will cost you."

The fish arrived that evening. In a bucket.

Grandpa was surprised. "What's the bucket for? I ordered carp, not a bucket."

"The bucket costs extra," retorted the veal lady. "The water is free. A Saint Nicholas' Day gift."

Grandpa scowled. "I expected carp steaks wrapped in paper, packed in ice."

"Ice? I don't carry ice. I'm a veal lady. I don't gut or fillet. This way, freshness is guaranteed. You want it or not?"

Grandpa passed her a small column of *zloty* coins. "I want it. This Christmas Eve, we eat carp before midnight mass. No German or Communist is going to tell me I can't eat the fish from Polish rivers. First they lived in my house, then they blew it up, then they built us this heartless block of concrete. But I will have my carp. You have to make a stand."

The veal lady rubbed Lucja's head, in sympathy for having a crazy grandfather. "Whatever you say, Kopec. You and the fish can make a stand together. Now I need my bucket if you don't mind."

Lucja hadn't heard a single word. There was a fish, in a bucket, in her house. A fish swimming in lazy eights, nosing the shiny metal. She followed her grandpa into the bathroom, where he dragged some sheets from the bath and emptied in the fish. It rolled from the bucket like a silver-brown tyre, then flapped for a bit until Lucja added some water.

"Now Mister Carp," she said, prodding his back. "Breathe all you like. Fish breathe water, Grandpa."

"Not for long," muttered Grandpa Kopec, trying to break the news in a roundabout way.

But Lucja wasn't interested in the hard facts of life. "He sucks the oxygen out with his gills, so we have to change the water every few days."

Grandpa's eyes widened. "He? It's a *he* now. And where did you learn so much about fish all of a sudden?"

Lucja looked up from the bath tub. "I *am* five, Grandpa. I *do* know stuff. I just don't know anything about history, 'cause you're the only one who cares about that."

Grandpa searched in his pocket for some tobacco. "Sometimes I think you're right," he said, heading outside for a smoke.

Lucja and the carp became very close. This was unusual, not because the creature in the bath was a fat brown fish, but because before this Lucja had never sat still for more than five seconds. Her mind wandered at the speed of light. Ideas ricocheted around in there like beads in a rattle and try as she might, she could never hold on to one for more than a moment. Often the beginnings and endings of her sentences would have no bearing on each other. For example:

"Mama, I am putting on my gloves because the whale song sounds so sad."

"Yes, Lucja," Mama would say, sometimes regretting that she could not recapture her child's beautiful world for herself.

So girl and fish became friends. Though possibly the fish didn't know a thing about it. He trawled his ceramic pool, never surprised to find titbits and left-overs that had not been there on his last revolution.

Lucja sat on a kettle box beside the tub talking to her new friend and nodding with great interest at his imagined replies.

"It is cold today, fishy," she would say, reaching a finger into the water to stroke the single fin on the carp's back. "I suppose you are cold all the time. Maybe you like the cold. Was it cold in your egg?"

And the fish would answer, but only in the child's world, "No, Lucja my dear. It was warm and soft and I wish I was there still.

But as I cannot be there, I am glad to be here, with you tickling my back and telling me important news of the outside world."

Lucja thought for a moment. "Important news. Hmm. Well, I saw a twig on the path today. It looked like a sparrow's leg. And the icicle on the fence has gone. Grandpa says one of the local ruffians may have snapped it off to use for mischief."

"Heavens!" gasped the carp. "Such news. The world is in such a state."

"And I have a hangnail," continued Lucja. "And this morning I woke up sneezing."

"Stop," cried the fish. "No more. I will be sad. Sing to me instead."

So Lucja sang a beautiful song about a cat who was using up his nine lives one by one. And the fish grew calm and his swimming grew lazy and slow.

This went on for two weeks.

"I cannot believe it," whispered Lucja's mother, Agata. "I thought she would lose interest. But she loves that carp. She sings to it. She's in there now cleaning the bathroom, *for the fish*."

Grandpa Feliks shrugged. "It has to go, Agata. It is Christmas Eve, and I will have fish. Neither Communists nor Germans, daughter. I am making a stand."

Agata sighed. "I know. You are right, of course. You better go in and tell her."

"M—me?" stuttered Feliks. "I thought that you would do the telling. Maybe whisk her to her room with a Christmas story."

Agata folded her arms. "*You* are the one making a stand, Papa. *You* can be the one to break her little heart."

Break her little heart? thought Feliks scowling. It was a fish in that bathtub, not a diamond necklace.

Lucja was showing the carp a drawing of the family when Feliks entered the bathroom.

"This is me and Mama and Grandpa. And there's you in the bath. I've given you a top hat because we're all going to the opera." The little girl noticed Feliks. "Oh, Grandpa, do you need to *go?*"

"Eh, no," said Feliks hurriedly. He was not comfortable with Lucja's policy of information-sharing concerning bathroom habits.

"I'll leave if you do," continued his granddaughter. "I know you need a lot of time, and a good book."

"No, it"s not that, Lucja. We need to talk about the carp."

"Fishy is his name, Grandpa."

"We need to talk about *Fishy.*"

"He's wonderful, isn't he? Maybe we can get a big bowl for

him, so we don't have to wash in the sink any more."

Grandpa scratched his chin, amazed to find that he was nervous. Decades of occupation, and a five-year-old made him nervous.

"You *do* know why we bought the carp... I mean, Fishy?"

Lucja turned to her grandfather. "I know we bought him to eat. But that was before. He's my friend now."

"But, Lucja, he's an *it*. It's a fish. Now you run along to your room and have a nap before midnight mass. Say goodbye to Fishy."

Tears stood out in the little girl's eyes. "No, Grandpa. He's mine now. You *can't* eat him."

Feliks did not take orders well. A fact that had cost him three years in a Soviet prison. "*Can't?* I will not be told *can't* in my own house. Not by Hitler. Not by Stalin. And not by you! That fish is my dinner. I will not be beaten again. I'm making a stand. Now, go to your room or I will kill the fish while you watch."

Lucja's tears flowed freely now, as she stared up at this man she thought she knew. But she was a Kopec, and so there was a spark of defiance in her.

"You are just like a Communist," she said to her Grandpa, then ran to her mother's apron.

Feliks wondered if it was possible to hate a fish. He was

beginning to feel it might be. All this trouble for a fillet of carp. It was ridiculous. Wasn't there a time when he and his brothers had fished the rivers freely, without fear of prosecution? Wasn't there a time when they threw small fish back, even medium-sized fish?

He felt a need to explain to Lucja that this was about more than fish. This was about freedom to enjoy the fruits of one's own country. This was about the realities of life. They were in Warsaw, not Washington.

Feliks steeled himself with deep breaths, then stomped down the corridor to the room his granddaughter shared with her mother.

He went in the door, talking.

"Now listen here, Lucja," he began, but the scolding withered in his throat. Lucja was already asleep. Her pillow was wet with tears. Feliks felt his resolve drain like water from a cracked vessel.

"Listen here, Lucja," he said, but softly this time.

His granddaughter lay sleeping, one eye half open in that strange way of hers. Her cheeks were red, he could see that even in the darkness. And her pointed chin was stolen from her grandmother. Feliks's wife.

This is highly unfair, thought Feliks. *What chance do I have?*

He saw Lucja for what she was. Innocent and happy. He

looked down on her with a sudden rush of love that filled his head with heat and set his hands trembling. It was as though the world had been made for her. Feliks reached down a single finger and touched her cheek.

The best argument of all, he thought. *How is an old rebel supposed to win? She will learn sorrow soon enough. Where is the harm in letting her be happy?*

Lucja opened the other eye. "I'm not asleep, you know. Just pretending because I'm cross with you."

"I see," said Feliks, feeling like a toothless bear. "Over Fishy?"

"Yes. He's my best friend, and I won't eat him."

Feliks sat on the corner of the bed. "How could you? He's your best friend."

Lucja knew she had the upper hand. "I bet I look like an angel when I'm pretending to be asleep."

"You do," admitted Grandpa. "Tomorrow you will look like a hungry angel."

"I don't care," cried Lucja, sitting up to hug her grandfather. "I will think about my head instead of my tummy. Thank you, Grandpa."

"It's not forever," said Feliks gruffly. "In a few days we will have to set him free. He will die in that bath."

He, thought the old man ruefully. *I'm calling the fish "he". Before you know it there'll be an extra place at the table.*

"Can Fishy stay until my birthday?"

Feliks was not good with dates. "When is that?"

"April."

"April? That's four months! We can't wash in the sink for four months."

"You could dig me a pond. In the green area."

"Are you crazy? How long do you think a carp would last in the green area? Other people aren't as fond of Fishy as we are."

"OK," said Lucja. "You win, Fishy stays in the bath."

"Thank you," said Feliks. "It's the only sensible thing. But not a day past your birthday. I'm serious. I'm taking a stand."

Feliks glanced up. Agata, his daughter, was at the door, smiling. Feliks wanted to smile too, but, of course, he could not.

"Now you, go to sleep. We will call you at eleven. And you, daughter, stop smiling like a simpleton and make me some strong coffee. One for the fish, too, while you're about it."

"Of course, Papa," said Agata. "You're the boss."

Feliks tucked in his granddaughter.

The boss, he thought. *I wish.*

Joe Craig

THE MENIDAKIS AFFAIR

Stuart's hands were always dry and as rough as any adult's. He'd been cleaning windows every school holiday since he was eight – just like his father and grandfather. That was a lot of windows. A lot of soap. In Stuart's eyes, twelve was the perfect age to retire. If only he could find a way to tell his dad.

He rushed ahead to ring the next bell. The sooner each job was finished, the better.

"You're in a hurry today," quipped his dad. Stuart ignored him and rang the bell again.

"Enough of that," his dad insisted. "This is Mrs Menidakis. She's probably asleep, poor dear."

Stuart was about to head for the next house in the row, but his dad was examining the front window. Smeared all the way down the glass was a black and white explosion of pigeon dropping.

"Let's get on with it anyway," said Stuart's dad. "The water we've got left over is clean enough. She can pay next time."

Without waiting for an answer, he planted his headphones on his ears. They were the old-fashioned type, with black foam pads. Stuart wondered how many windows it took before you could afford an iPod.

"I'll go round the back," he called out. His dad was singing along to the hiss in his ears. Stuart reached the side gate with his bucket in one hand and his ladder over his shoulder. Mrs Menidakis always left the gate open.

"Careful back there," his dad shouted, far too loud. "Her conservatory has one of them flimsy roofs, remember. Any trouble, give me a whistle."

Stuart didn't answer. He clattered down the side of the house falling deeper into his frustration. His dad never remembered that he couldn't whistle.

He set about the conservatory windows with a sigh, plunging his fists into the cold, grey froth. He even hated the smell of it now. He finished the ground floor in no time and snatched up the ladder. The conservatory jutted out of the back of the house, so to get to the first floor windows you had to walk on its roof. Trouble was, the roof was just a sheet of reinforced plastic. Whoever built it certainly wasn't thinking of the window cleaners.

He sloshed his rag on to the bedroom window. The muscles in his arm tensed up. Something wasn't right. It didn't bother him that the curtains were drawn; that made sense if Mrs Menidakis was having a nap. Then he realised: the outside of the glass was warm.

He took a step back and noticed his reflection was illuminated. A glow radiated from behind the curtains. In the centre, where they didn't quite meet, there was a sliver of luminous green. Stuart shuffled towards it, fixated by the light. When he was close enough he pressed his nose to the window pane and peeked through the crack.

His eyes weren't used to the brightness, but he could pick out hazy shadows and the outlines of furniture. He blinked fast, almost mesmerised. If he stared for more than a second it stung his eyes, but he was desperate to find out what was causing the glow.

Suddenly, his vision was blocked. Stuart jumped. The breath froze in his throat. A face stared back at him from inside the room – a bright white face, right up close to his own. Stuart tried to look away, but the man's eyes had him transfixed. They were so pale they were almost white themselves, blending into his skin. This was *not* Mrs Menidakis.

At last, Stuart stepped away from the window. Too late. The man opened it and growled,

"What are you doing?"

His voice was pure gravel. He leaned out, grabbing at Stuart, a grimace splitting his face. Stuart jumped to the side, out of reach, his back against the window. In the sunlight Stuart could see just how pale this man was. It was as if someone had rubbed flour into him – even his hair was a shocking white.

"I'm the window cleaner," Stuart gabbled. "Me and my dad, we…"

He trailed off. The man was climbing out of the window. Stuart gasped at the size of his arms. They were as thick as the drainpipe.

"Dad!" Stuart shouted, but he knew his father wouldn't hear him. He pushed himself up against the house. "We're just the window cleaners. We come every four months." The words tumbled out of his mouth. "Mrs Menidakis knows us. Ask Mrs Menidakis."

The man wasn't very much taller than Stuart, but he was three times as wide. The green glow from the window illuminated his features, brighter and more hideous with every step he took towards Stuart.

"There is no Mrs Menidakis," the man hissed.

Stuart felt his stomach jump into his chest. His instinct was to cry out for help. Only air escaped his lips. He was trapped.

The man lunged at him.

Stuart reached towards his only way of escape – up. He clasped the guttering above him. It broke away immediately. Stuart half-fell, kicking over his bucket. Soapy water flooded across the conservatory roof. The man lurched towards him, but slipped and fell on his back with a splat. Stuart clawed his way up on to the tiles. If he could get over to the front of the house he could attract his dad's attention – or anyone's.

He reached for the TV aerial and hauled himself up. He was going to make it. But something clamped around his ankle. He glanced behind him. With a fist the size of a football, the man was dragging Stuart back.

"Help!" Stuart screamed, his arm straining at its socket. Was there anybody around to hear him?

He couldn't hold on any more. All the strength drained from his body. The man pulled him back with a rough tug. Stuart bumped along the tiles, scraping his chin. Then the man grabbed him by the back of the neck and slung him over his shoulder.

Stuart was hardly aware of anything now, except the green light. The heat of it made his face itch. And then there was this burly man, carrying him in a fireman's lift across the roof of the conservatory.

"If you are just a window cleaner, you are unfortunate," the man whispered. "I cannot take that risk. Not now that you have seen it." He pounded across the roof. "It wasn't such a long way to fall, people will say. Only a metre and a half, they'll say. What a shame he had to go and fall on his head."

Stuart knew he was going to die. He closed his eyes and let his whole body turn limp. But then he heard something. A low creak. The noise shot into Stuart's brain. It was the roof of the conservatory, giving in under the load.

Just a few more seconds, thought Stuart. He kicked out wildly, catching the man by surprise. At the same time he reached round the man's head, feeling for his eyes and clinging to his face. The man spun round, trying to throw Stuart off, but he couldn't. He veered away from the edge, obviously not wanting to fall himself.

Come on, thought Stuart, suddenly awash with determination. He wished there was some way to make himself heavier. But he didn't need it. A fat, suburban pigeon swooped down and landed on the roof. Stuart froze for an instant. He held his breath. Then...

CRACK!

The man lurched backwards, losing his grip on Stuart. The

conservatory roof split right down the middle. The next thing Stuart knew, he was crashing to the floor. All he could see were splinters of plastic – and the earth rushing towards him.

THUMP!

He hit the ground face first. His jaw crunched together, but he didn't black out. He rolled over and realised why. Beneath him was the perfect cushion – a huge ball of human muscle. The man hadn't been so lucky. His chalky face beamed straight up at the sky, eyes closed. He was unconscious. The pigeon perched on the edge of the hole, watching a drip.

Stuart staggered to his feet just as his dad rushed round to the back of the house. His face was twisted in horror. His headphones trailed behind him on the patio. He rattled the conservatory door, but it was locked.

"Are you OK?" he shouted, hammering on the glass.

Stuart looked around, bemused. He examined the hole above him, then the man at his feet.

"Let me in," his dad cried. He unclipped a mobile phone from his belt. Stuart snapped out of his daze.

"Wait," he shouted.

His dad froze, then his thumb quivered over the 9 button. He couldn't have looked more puzzled. Stuart nudged the white-faced man with his foot. A groan escaped his lungs, but he was definitely unconscious.

"What happened?" Stuart's dad yelled. Stuart was looking in the other direction. He could see the stairs. At the top was the lurid green glow, creeping down towards him. Stuart's mind was racing. Why had the man been so upset? It was one thing to go ballistic if someone peeks through your curtains, quite another to try dumping that person headfirst off a rooftop. He was hiding something special up there.

"What are you doing?" Stuart's dad called out.

Stuart didn't look round. He put a hand up behind him and edged one step towards the stairs. Only then did he glance over his shoulder. His dad was gripping the phone so tight it looked like the plastic might melt.

Finally, Stuart knew what to say:

"If I need you, I'll whistle."

THE MAGICIAN'S DAUGHTER

Annie Dalton

Wildwhistle, Wolverine & sons,
22 Cross Street, Pelham Market, Middle
Ambria

Dear wich,
I hop you are well? We are doing koldruns on
speshul offer now. You shuld get sum whil their going
cheep!
yr respeckful servant
Bertie Wildwhistle Esq.

Bertie's first ever business letter had been written on official Wildwhistle's stationery, when he was just six years old. Aunt Pearl had shown him how to address an envelope and taught him how to fold his letter exactly two and a half times to make it fit, then he licked the envelope and put it proudly in her out-tray. For years he believed his aunt had posted it with the other real grownup letters. In fact she had pasted it into a special album along with a photograph of him taken in front of the family department store, looking slightly worried in his outsized flannel trousers.

WILDWHISTLE, WOLVERINE & SONS Magical Supplies. Est 1699 said a sign over a rather grand striped awning. In the background an old fashioned milk float was just chugging into view.

With its air of being stuck in a sleepy 1950s time-warp, Pelham Market seemed quaint to visitors from non-magical regions. Quaint but not too alarmingly magic. You'd have to go to North Ambria these days to find real magic or (if you had some kind of death wish!) to the dangerous, nameless regions beyond.

Pelham Market hadn't always been so tame. Mungo Wildwhistle, one of Bertie's ancestors (a bit of a black sheep, according to the aunts) had actually gone off to seek his fortune. His old leather knapsack still hung behind the door of the staff kitchen, peppered with mysterious scorch marks. Bertie would touch it secretly and wonder.

Some people might think there was something depressing about running a magical supplies store in a town where magic levels were dropping steadily with every passing day. But Bertie never allowed himself this thought. It would have seemed too disloyal after all the aunts had done for him.

The Wildwhistle sisters were already in their eighties by the time he joined their household. They had no experience of small children, but they loved pale puzzled little Bertie fiercely, warding off germs and bad influences (like the Tooley boys), religiously spooning cod liver oil into him, imprisoning him in layers of prickly Fairisle and flannel to keep out the winter chill.

Bertie understood, without it ever being said, that when the aunts retired, he would follow the Wildwhistle tradition and take over running the shop. Until that day came, they made it their duty to teach their nephew everything they had ever learned from their father Stanley Wildwhistle, who had learned it from *his* father William Copper Wildwhistle, and so on back through the generations.

When he was small, Bertie was happy to come to work with his aunts, instead of going to school like normal children. He actually enjoyed polishing brass and dusting mirrors, because while he was doing it he was breathing in Wildwhistle's special smell of old wood and lavender polish — and yes, *magic*; magic which came shivering and whispering out of the ancient walls like a secret promise only Bertie could hear.

And, just once or twice, his patience had been rewarded.

One bright windy morning in early spring, a witch came spinning into Wildwhistles and Wolverines' department store via its old fashioned, not terribly reliable, revolving door. To everyone's horror it stuck half way. Before one of the great aunts could rush to help, the witch gabbled a string of foreign-sounding words. The door began to revolve — but at twice its normal speed. Like a pea from a peashooter, the witch was catapulted into the store, laughing and breathless.

She gazed around her with strangely clear green eyes, Bertie remembered years later, more like a curious child than an adult, trailing long pale fingers over the displays. It was impossible to know how old she was; her mischievous face was completely unlined. She wore wild violets, white ones as well as purple, braided into her tangled black locks. Bertie could still smell them long after she'd gone.

Perhaps it was something about that spring, because he saw his first (and last) giant just a few days later. Bertie and the aunts actually heard him before they saw him, setting all the buildings in Cross Street shuddering with his unsteady lumbering tread.

"That'll be Giant Blunderblast," sighed Aunt Ruby. "I expect his boots are shot. Must be thirty years since he bought that last pair."

"Did he seemed a bit confused to you that time?" Aunt Emerald asked her sister, as if it had been just last week.

Aunt Ruby made tutting sounds. "Yes, poor old boy. It comes to us all."

A thunderous sound went off, like ten dinner gongs clanging at once, as Giant Blunderblast heaved on the special bell-pull outside.

Aunt Emerald hurried to let him in through a side entrance which had apparently been built with giants in mind. Aunt Ruby fetched a pair of immense leather boots from the storeroom, wrapping each boot exquisitely in tissue and brown paper.

"Isn't he going to try them on?" whispered Bertie who'd been peeping at the giant from a safe distance.

Aunt Ruby shook her head. "He always buys the same kind. He's old you see, Bertie. Old people tend to get set in their ways."

Bertie's eyes popped out on stalks when he saw old Blunderblast produce handfuls of real gold coins to pay for his purchase. Aunt Ruby had to pick out the correct amount, explaining what she was doing, so he'd know she wasn't trying to cheat him.

Aunt Pearl was too shy to deal with customers directly. She sat in the office from nine to five helping Mr Prewitt with the mail order sales.

When Bertie got bored with writing imaginary business letters, he was sometimes allowed to leaf through old business letters which his Wildwhistle ancestors had filed away over the years. The deceptively dull-seeming cabinets were crammed with unexpected treasures: salt-stained, faintly fish-smelling messages from a tribe of Mer People located somewhere in the Caribbean; a half-charred demand for supplies which gave off a bitter whiff of dragon fire.

These glimpses of vanished and vastly more magical times made Bertie feel jealous that he'd missed Wildwhistles in its glory days. By the time he arrived to live with the aunts, most of their custom came from coach parties of sightseers from East Ambria. They liked to try on the invisibility cloaks, sniggering as various bits of them disappeared. Afterwards, they'd go on up the hill to the Fairytale Museum to try their hand at mixing enchanted potions, before they went back home to their central heating and flat screen TVs.

As he grew older, Bertie became distinctly less enchanted at the prospect of making mirrors sparkle for customers who rarely put in an appearance.

When he turned thirteen, he went through a rebel phase;

demanding blue jeans instead of flannels, and flatly refusing to wear any garment with a Fairisle pattern. Against the expressed wishes of his aunts, Bertie started hanging around the Kardomah coffee bar on his afternoons off. As the Tooley boys filled him in on the dramatic changes in the outside world, he became restless and at times cruel.

"If you don't get computerised, you're limiting yourselves to local demand," he lectured his bewildered aunts. "I mean, what customers have you got, really? A senile old giant and a toothless couple of dragons who couldn't raise a flame if you gave them a can of petrol. But if you got a website you'd pull in the international market. Seriously, you'd be laughing!" he added defiantly, imitating the Tooley brothers' careless way of talking.

The aunts were so hurt they didn't speak to him for a week.

Bertie was appalled at his own ingratitude. It wasn't the aunts' fault if the magic was slowly draining out of Middle Ambria, leaving Wildwhistles high and dry. It was pointless trying to bully them into changing with the times. Like the giant they were too set in their ways. Bertie just had to help them survive whatever happened next.

Wildwhistles held out for another two years, but by that time takings had dropped to an all-time low. To the aunts' distress and shame, they were forced to sell out to Frank Folly's Magimart chain.

At the solicitors they shakily signed their names.

"But Wildwhistles was meant for you Bertie!" Aunt Ruby wept. "It was meant for you!"

The night before the store was due to close, Bertie had a strange dream. He was alone on a narrow moonlit road. Like a shining thread it wound its way into the distance, past rushing streams and cone-shaped hills where wild apple trees grew. On the tallest hill, floating above the apple orchards, was a strange glimmering castle. As soon as he saw it, Bertie knew he was looking into a faraway kingdom which had somehow kept its magic.

He jerked awake to hear Aunt Ruby tapping on his door. "Rise and shine, Bertie, dear!" she called brightly.

"Righty ho," he called back, but he was stunned and confused.

He'd only just realised that he'd been dreaming that same dream for years; but for some reason this was the first time he'd remembered it on waking.

It must mean something, he thought with a twinge of hope, *that I remembered it today of all days?*

He angrily squashed down this thought. He'd wasted too many years waiting and hoping. It was just too late. Nothing was going to save the aunts or their vanished world, not now, not ever.

Simply getting washed and dressed seemed to take all Bertie's energy. He felt as if he had an imaginary crow hopping behind him, cawing, *last time, last time.*

Downstairs the aunts waited with tremulous smiles to see him off. They were too frail nowadays to work in the shop. Bertie had been running the business, what was left of it, for months, with help from Mr Prewitt's daughter, Milly.

As if it was any other day, Bertie bent down so Aunt Pearl could adjust his tie, then he stooped over Aunt Emerald's wheelchair to let her brush invisible lint from his jacket. Last of all, Aunt Ruby stretched up on tiptoe to push back the lock of Bertie's hair which stubbornly refused to lie flat.

Last time, last time, cawed the invisible crow as Bertie took the keys from the hook in the hall and left the house.

He walked through the early morning streets feeling as if his legs had turned to lead. This day had been looming for so long, and now he couldn't seem to picture a life on the other side.

Eventually he arrived outside the still-oddly-imposing green and gold frontage of Wildwhistles, Wolverine & Sons.

The aunts had never been able to tell him the identity of that mysterious "Wolverine"; or wouldn't, more like, he thought with a sudden, faintly mischievous smile.

Bertie unlocked a side door and breathed in Wildwhistles' unique smell. Ancient wood, lavender polish — and still, but very faintly, magic.

Milly Prewitt arrived exactly five minutes later – out of loyalty Bertie thought gratefully. There wasn't really that much for her to do. In his grandfather's day, Wildwhistles had occupied all four floors of its rambling premises; now it had shrunk to two.

Not knowing what else to do, they set to work as usual. They steam-pressed the few remaining ball dresses, checked invisibility cloaks for moth holes, vacuumed flying carpets and buffed up a display of ancient amulets (carefully disabling them first).

At ten thirty they took a break.

"What will happen to it all?" Milly asked forlornly, dunking her ginger biscuit.

Bertie shrugged. "They'll probably ship it all up the road to the Fairy Tale Museum for the tourists. What will you do?" he asked her, suddenly guilty that he hadn't bothered to find this out. "Will you work for Magimart?'

"Hardly!" Milly spluttered. "Can you see me in a fairy costume, with these hips!" She gave him a sisterly pat. "What about you, Bertie?"

"No idea," he said gloomily. "I might end up working for Magimart myself."

Milly gestured at the knapsack behind the kitchen door. "Maybe you should just go off like Mungo and seek your fortune," she teased, trying to cheer him up.

At two thirty Bertie sent Milly home with her wages.

At five thirty on the dot, he locked the doors and went around turning off lights. Not knowing what to do next, he sat on the bottom stair in the silent shadowy store.

Memories floated back of a younger, more hopeful Bertie.

We have got koldruns on speshul offer now, he remembered wistfully.

Bertie leaned his head against the carved oak bannisters. Worn out from the weeks of worry, he must have dozed off.

He woke to see an enormous shadow blotting out the street light.

There was a massive splintering of glass. Glittering fragments rained down on Bertie as a flying white horse came sailing into the store, stopping fractionally too late to avoid the ball-gowns. Like a circus tent at the end of the show, the entire display collapsed inward.

Bertie sat transfixed and speechless; partly because Wildwhistles had been wrecked on its last day, but mostly because it was the first time he had ever seen a flying horse.

He heard impatient ripping sounds as the rider blindly tore her way out through priceless rose pink silk. She swung herself down from the saddle and began to soothe the horse, which was trembling violently. "You brave boy," the girl said lovingly. "Don't worry, you'll never have to do that again."

It was still young, Bertie realised, more of a flying colt really.

There was a lot to be surprised about just at that moment: the girl's strange pale candyfloss hair, the fact that she was riding a horse with wings – that and the fact that she was here at all. But Bertie was particularly surprised to see her wearing a mud-stained ball gown in a style Wildwhistles had discontinued well over a hundred years ago. She had to haul it up in handfuls, he saw, so as not to trip on the hem.

"I wonder where they keep the wands," she muttered, looking around distractedly.

"First floor," Bertie said, snapping on the nearest light.

The girl gave a squeak of fright. "What are *you* doing here!"

Bertie should have been asking *her* that but he just said calmly, "I work here, or I used to. It's my last day." He surveyed the ruined ball-gown display and to his surprise, he laughed.

He showed her up to the first floor. Since it wasn't Wildwhistles' policy to leave power objects lying around for just anyone who happened to come by on a flying horse, the wands were kept in a locked case – locked with magic charms, that is.

He spoke the words of release silently in his head as he'd been taught, waiting for that tiny telltale click, then he opened the case and took out the most powerful wand of the three.

"It's not very flash. But it's the best one by miles."

Bertie tried to hand her the wand, but she looked alarmed.

"Oh, no, they said I have to pay you first!"

She rushed back downstairs. Bertie followed with the wand, feeling as if he was having his lifetime's supply of surprises in one night.

His next surprise left him breathless.

Rummaging through a saddle bag, the girl brought out sparkling handfuls of jewels. "Is that enough?" she asked anxiously. "Obviously I'd want to pay for the window."

Bertie almost laughed. Was it *enough*?

He hastily shook his head. "I mean, yes it's enough, but you may as well just have it. You're obviously in some kind of trouble."

To his dismay the girl burst into tears.

"I'm just a bit tired," she sobbed, when she could speak. "I'm not usually this weedy!"

"Don't move," Bertie told her.

He ran up to the kitchen, coming back with a clean mug and an old magic kettle. "I loved this when I was little," he grinned. "You just say what you want and it'll…"

He saw her face light up with recognition. "Chicken soup!" she commanded. The air filled with the savoury smell of chicken and vegetables.

He should have guessed that a girl with a flying horse would know what to do with a magic kettle.

Bertie sat under the stern gaze of his Wildwhistle ancestors, watching a strange girl in a ball-dress slurping up enchanted soup, with less than perfect table manners.

She was chattering away now, giving the impression she'd been starved of company for years. "He's just a baby still, my horse," she explained with her mouth full. "He can only fly a hundred leagues in one day."

A hundred leagues seemed a fair distance to Bertie, who had never gone further than five miles from Pelham Market.

"I don't know why they left him in the stables when they took all the others. Maybe they thought he wasn't useful because he was just a foal?"

She seemed to think Bertie must know who "they" were.

"I've been training him for ages," she added, with a toss of her strange pale hair. "They stole all the power objects from the castle. That's why I had to come to Wildwhistles. It was the only way I could think of to break the enchantment."

Bertie was starting to feel dizzy. "Maybe you could tell me from the beginning," he suggested gently.

The girl drained the last of her soup. "My parents got caught up in a magic war," she explained. "Some magicians blew my parents to smithereens and put a shrinking spell on my sisters. Mum had just put me down for a nap, under an invisibility cloak, luckily, or they'd have shrunk me too."

"They *shrank* your sisters?" Bertie gasped.

She showed him, matter of factly, with her finger and thumb. "They hate it." Her voice shook with sudden emotion. "They especially hate sounding like tiny mice when they talk. We racked our brains, but we couldn't think of a way to reverse the spell. Then I found some old invoices from Wildwhistles and that's when I got the idea to come and get a magic wand."

He saw her try to smother a yawn. Bertie could see she was swaying with exhaustion where she sat.

"Why don't you grab a nap," he suggested. "An hour more or less isn't going to make any difference now. Then you can use the wand to get yourself back to…?"

"Azure Rood," she mumbled rubbing her eyes.

He blinked away a glimmering castle floating above moonlit apple trees. Azure Rood was the northernmost point of North Ambria, before the dangerous nameless magical regions began. The same land, he guessed, that those murderous magicians came from.

"If you change your mind about the jewels—" Without finishing her sentence, the girl lay down next to the cauldron display and was asleep in seconds. In a sort of slow-motion origami, the horse folded up its wings, then its legs, and rested warily beside his mistress, watching Bertie with its beautiful liquid brown eyes.

Bertie fetched a warm cloak from the store room, just a normal regular cloak, to cover her while she slept.

He picked up the wand and felt its hidden power tingle against his palm. It occurred to him that he had dusted power objects and arranged them in displays; he had even sold them overseas to mail-order customers. What he'd never dared to do, even as a magic obsessed little boy, was to *use* one. Bertie wasn't sure if this thought made him want to laugh or cry.

Like the magician's daughters, he'd been under a shrinking spell, he realised with shocked surprise. The inexperienced aunts had been so scared he might come to harm, they'd tried too hard to keep him safe; and like a hazel nut inside its shell, Bertie's spirit had secretly started to shrivel.

But tonight magic had come smashing its way into his life, in the shape of a wild girl on a flying horse, and set him free.

He only wished he could do more to help her in return.

Magic soup, a free wand, that's nothing, he thought fiercely. This girl had virtually brought herself up. She'd single-handedly trained a magical beast, and just set off into the blue, trusting that she'd somehow find a way to save her sisters. *But what if it doesn't work out?* he thought anxiously.

Suppose the wand didn't, actually, restore the girls family to their normal size? Did she even have a fallback plan? Bertie somehow doubted it.

He realised he was looking around Wildwhistles as if he might not be seeing it again any time soon. Suddenly the shop seemed painfully dear to him. That was when Bertie knew he was leaving his old life behind.

On his way to the office, he stepped over the saddle bags which spilled out their outrageous treasures as freely as wild flowers.

"If you change your mind about the jewels—" he heard her say in his head.

Just one duck-egg sized diamond would buy back Wildwhistles and keep the aunts in luxury for the rest of their lives.

"Yes," he whispered daringly to the sleeping girl. "Yes, I've changed my mind."

Closeted in his office, Bertie made two brief phone calls; one to his aunts' solicitors, the other to a surprised Milly Prewitt who cheerfully agreed to mind the aunts until Bertie came back.

Finally he took down Mungo's knapsack from its hook, then he went through Wildwhistles like a silent whirlwind, throwing in all the portable magical objects he could find. Then, with a beating heart, he waited for the magician's daughter to wake up.

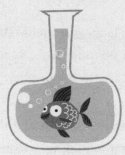

I REMEMBER

Chris d' Lacey

I once read an article about an interesting man called Joe Brainard. Joe was an artist. Among the many things he did was to write a book called I Remember, *which was just snippets of his memories, all beginning with the phrase,* I remember. *Sometimes during a school visit I ask children to have a try at writing their own. It can be very interesting because each memory is often a little story in itself. Here are some of mine. Not all are from my childhood, but most are. They range from funny to sad to scary to bizarre. Have a read, then have a go yourself...*

I remember England winning the World Cup in 1966. I kept rushing back and forth into my Grandma's kitchen to tell her the score. She was washing clothes on an old scrubbing board and couldn't give a stuff.

I remember standing at a hospital window watching fireworks exploding outside. I was five. I was in for a hernia operation. I'd ruptured myself trying to pick up a suitcase while my dad was loading up the car for us to go on holiday. We never made the holiday.

I remember the thunder of steam trains as they shook the platform on the station at the top of my estate. I was frightened of them and thought they were alive.

I remember my Alsatian dog, Bruce, stealing the Sunday joint off the top of the cooker. He devoured it in minutes and was banished to his garden kennel for a week.

I remember doing the scoring for my village cricket team and desperately wanting to win the neatest scorebook award at the end of the season. It always went to a man called Derek, who used a graphite pencil as dark as a black sausage and made dots as big as raindrops in his book.

I remember being chased across a field by a horse. It ran me all the way into a ditch and kept me there for half an hour.

I remember sunburn and how the flakes of red skin used to peel like onion layers off the back of my neck. In those days, no one ever carped about the ozone hole and cricketers never put sun cream on their noses.

I remember playing a game called fairy footsteps in the street.

I remember catching sticklebacks in the brook at the bottom of the same street.

I remember seeing a mole above ground one day. I was playing football with my mates. A few of us gathered round the creature, which looked dreadfully confused. None of us knew what to do. Then a bully came steaming up and punted it ten yards between the jumpers we'd put down for goalposts, killing it. I was sickened and couldn't play on.

I remember being knocked out by my sister, Lynsy. I was carrying her in my arms and dropped her on her bed. As she bounced, her knee came up and whacked me under the chin. For three seconds I was euphoric, out of my body, on the ceiling. I came back with a massive thud of pain.

I remember dyeing my hair gold when I was seventeen. The girls at school thought it was brilliant. My form teacher said I looked like "a clown". He gave me a suspension.

I remember the way my dad used to wake me at 4 a.m. on a cold winter's morning. He would clamp his hand around my ankle like the devil. When I jolted awake he would say: "There's toast on the table. If you want to come with me in the lorry today I'm leaving in half an hour." I never missed.

I remember seeing a naked man running down the street. I was eight, in the cab of my dad's lorry. Shocked, he gasped, "Did you see that?" clearly hoping I hadn't. Yet he drove determinedly after the bloke for about half a minute.

I remember my English teacher telling me I didn't have a creative thought in my head.

I remember being inspired to write my first song. I hummed it over and over on the bus coming home from school. I sprinted in, grabbed my guitar and worked out the chord sequence. The lyrics went: "I'm just a boy who likes TV, but now T Rex (*a very ancient pop group*) mean more to me…" I never completed it.

I remember falling to my knees and sobbing into a tea towel the last time I put Duke, my ginger cat, to bed. He had an inoperable tumour. The vet came at 11:00 the next morning and put him to sleep.

I remember working on a night-shift, making toilet rolls to pay my way through my A-level exams.

I remember the time I saw a dead body in my grandad's coffin store. I was petrified. He'd been an undertaker for thirty years and was used to the odd stiff. He rubbed my shoulder and said, "Don't fret, lad. It's only the living that can hurt you."

I remember seeing the film *Zulu* seven times.

I remember the Christmas that my brother and I were both given a spirograph as our main present. Major disappointment!

I remember missing an open goal from five yards out in a schools cup semi-final. We lost the game and I was crushed. No one would speak to me for days.

I remember climbing to the top of the Scott Monument in Edinburgh. I met two Japanese tourists who asked me to take their photograph. I tried to explain that it was pointless because all I could see behind them was sky. I took the shot but it could have been anywhere: Edinburgh, the Arctic, Tokyo City...

I remember nicking shillings from the sideboard drawer. They were for the electricity meter. I spent them on bars of chocolate.

I remember Norway and my "Uncle" Sigard. He lived on an island in the middle of a fjord. He spoke no English, me no Norwegian. We spent a week together, talking in grunts and signs. He'd been a fighter in the Norwegian resistance during World War II. He showed me his gun, his knives, his camouflage dress and how to travel about an island without being spotted. Best holiday I ever had.

I remember my dad taking weeks to build me a go-kart. On my first journey I went fifteen yards, hit a lamppost, buckled the front axle, bust my lip and caused a car to swerve into another. My mum said to my dad, "No more go-karts."

I remember my first visit to a publisher, in Knightsbridge, a very posh region of London. Unsure of the dress code, I wore my only suit and tie. Everyone else was in jeans and T-shirts. My editor said, "Are you going on somewhere afterwards?" She might just as well have stamped the word "novice" on my forehead.

I remember my mother screaming: "Stop blinking!" from my bedroom window when I was playing outside with my mates.

I remember Subbuteo, the best football game ever invented.

I remember, while playing Subbuteo, always being distracted by my best friend's lava lamp. He later confessed that he only switched it on to put me off. No wonder I never won the league.

I remember buying Sports Mixtures from a sweet shop on my way to school in the mornings. They were four for a penny. The day the shop closed down, I went in and handed over my penny with an air of glum resignation. The shopkeeper smiled and gave me the rest of the box, approximately three hundred sweets.

I remember my mother asking me three times who would I go with if she and my dad ever got divorced. Twice I said, "You, Mum." When eventually they did split up, I chose my dad.

I remember my dad taking me to Trafalgar Square to see Nelson's

Column. There were lots of pigeons. He made me stand with my arms out and covered them with bird seed. Pretty soon I was covered with pigeons. I was frightened of birds for eighteen more years until...

I remember finding an injured pigeon, who came to be known as Gregory Peck, in my local park and nursing him back to health. It cured my phobia about birds. Not long ago, I buried his last surviving relative, Scruffy, just outside the shed they'd used as a pigeon loft for twenty-two years...

I remember, during one Chemistry lesson at school, me and my mates filling up a clean acid bottle with water and putting a goldfish in it. My Chemistry teacher wasn't impressed. He made us stay behind afterwards and calculate how many goldfish it would take to fill the school swimming pool.

I remember throwing up on a cross channel ferry. I reached out for what I thought was a straw basket and yakked into a posh schoolgirl's straw boater! My mate quickly threw it overboard and no one was any the wiser.

I remember wading through a sea of acorns on a leafy avenue in Bromley one autumn afternoon. The decision to gather some up and feed them to the tame squirrels I used to see in the library gardens there was a turning point in my life — but I wouldn't know it for another twenty-three years, until I wrote a book called *The Fire Within*.

Helen Dunmore

THE BLUE GARDEN

"Doesn't it look peaceful?" someone said
as our train halted on the embankment.
There was nothing to do but gaze
at the blue garden

where blue roses slowly opened,
blue apples glistened
beneath the spreading peacock of leaves

and the fountain spat jets of pure Prussian.
The decking was made with fingers of midnight
the grass was as blue as Kentucky,

even the children playing
in their ultramarine paddling-pool
were touched by a blue Midas

who had changed their skin
from the warm colours of earth
to the azure of heaven.

"Don't they look happy?" someone said,
as the train manager apologised
for the inconvenience caused to our journey,

and yes, they looked happy.
Didn't we wish we were in the blue garden
soaked in a spray of lapis lazuli

didn't we wish we could dig in the cobalt earth
for sky-coloured potatoes,
didn't we wish our journey was over

and we were free to race down the embankment
and be caught up in the blue, like those children
who soon shrank to dots of cerulean
as our train got going.

Jackie French

FROG

The lane behind the museum smelt of old beer and garbage cans from the Commercial Hotel across the way.

Quong Tart Lane the sign at the corner said. The lane looked like it hadn't changed in a hundred years.

It probably hadn't.

Louise kicked the pile of rubble on the footpath. The hotel looked like a mob of drunks had been at it with hammers. It was just being renovated, Mum had said. The mess would be cleaned up sometime.

Biscuit Creek time, Louise reckoned. The hotel looked like it had been there for a hundred years as well.

Everything about Biscuit Creek was old. Everything that mattered anyway. The shops were old, the streets were old, wide enough to turn a bullock team around in. Even the school looked more like a convict prison than a school. It had probably looked exactly the same when Mum went there.

"Nothing ever changes much in Biscuit Creek..."

Who said that? Louise glanced around.

It wasn't Mum's voice. Mum was still yakking over the teapot in the museum with Mrs Halibut, and the hotel windows on this side were high and small. Quong Tart Lane was just a dead end. Just like Biscuit Creek, a dead end that lead to nowhere...

"And that, of course, was what Frog hated about the town. She thought Biscuit Creek was a nowhere place, where nothing ever happened. But all things change, of course, and later it was this very factor that..."

Louise stepped around the rubble and peered around the corner into the backyard of the hotel.

There was a tour bus in the centre of the yard, over by the empty kegs, a small one, a twenty seater perhaps. It was empty, the tourists clustered around the tour guide. She was Mum's age maybe, in jeans and T-shirt with some sort of logo on the front, bright green like her cap.

It was a dumb sort of cap, thought Louise. It had two flaps

like frog's legs over each ear and another two flaps to keep her neck warm down the back.

"Frog arrived here in…" The guide paused as she saw Louise. Her expression was hard to read. Then she smiled. "Hello," she said.

"Hello," said Louise. "Are you here to see the museum?"

The guide shook her head, the bright green flaps bobbing at her ears. "No. We're just on a tour of the town."

"But Mum wasn't expecting… I mean, she's supposed to do the historical tours, but we only arrived this morning and…"

"Your mother's the new museum curator?" The woman sounded strangely excited. Her accent was odd. Nothing you could put your finger on. Just odd.

Louise nodded. "Yeah, she grew up here. Mum got made redundant from the bank in Sydney last year so…" She stopped. What business was it of theirs why they'd moved here? She should learn to keep her mouth shut.

"That's all right, Nienza." The woman smiled, almost, thought Louise, as though she understood without having to be told. "I'm giving the tour today. Would you like to join us?"

Why was she calling her Nienza? Someone muttered something, too low for Louise to make it out. They sounded excited, too, a sort of suppressed excitement like bubbles in a bottle waiting to be let out. Surely no one could be that excited over a tour of Biscuit Creek.

Louise wondered how to decline politely.

"Well, I—"

"Come on, Nienza, do. If you've just arrived today it will give you a chance to see the town. You start school on Monday? It will give you a chance to learn your way around."

She has a point, thought Louise. Mum had driven her round the town this morning, but it was too quick to take in much. And Monday was going to be tough enough. Besides, she'd unpacked already. What else was there to do in Biscuit Creek on Saturday afternoons?

"OK," said Louise. The tour guide grinned. Someone murmured again, more excited than ever. The group began to climb back into the bus, as though this was the signal they'd been waiting for.

"You can sit beside me, Nienza," said the tour guide, settling into the driver's seat. She must be the driver too, realised Louise.

"My name's not Nienza. It's Louise," said Louise.

The tour guide laughed. "Louise. Of course. Nienza is just a pet name – like honey or sweetheart. I'm sorry if you don't like it."

"Oh, I don't mind," said Louise. She settled into the seat beside the guide as the engine barked into life.

Out of the lane behind the hotel, past the museum.

"And as I was saying," continued the tour guide, "that is the museum on our left. It was originally the Literary Institute, then the Oddfellows Hall, finally falling into disrepair before being renovated by the newly formed Biscuit Creek Historical Association. Up the main street now. That's the swimming pool on your right. It was built in 1972, but not opened until two years later, as the concrete supplied had been poor quality and had to be repaired. The swimming pool was there in Frog's day, but there is no record that Frog was much of a swimmer... That's the park beyond it. You can see the children on the swings – the swings are new, put in only last year, the money raised by a committee from cake stalls..."

Oh, yeah, fascinating, thought Louise. She was already sorry she'd come.

"And the wooden fort was donated by Lamb's Drapery, we'll pass that in a minute. Frog was probably too old to have played in the park, though like the rest of Biscuit Creek it was part of the tapestry of her life." The guide changed gears as they went up the hill.

"Who's Frog?" whispered Louise.

The tour guide glanced at her. Someone giggled just behind them.

"Frog was the greatest Prime Minister our country has ever known." The guide's voice seemed totally sincere.

"I've never heard of him."

The tour guide grinned again. "Her, Nienza. Frog was a woman."

"I never knew we'd had a woman Prime Minister!"

"You don't like studying history, then?"

Louise shook her head. "It's boring. History never changes."

The guide's grin grew even wider at that. "Perhaps not, Nienza. But sometimes what we know about the past can change. Sometimes how we look at our history can change. And history is the doorstep to tomorrow."

Louise shrugged. "It's still boring. Mum likes it, though," she glanced round guiltily. "I'm sorry. I'm interrupting your talk."

"It doesn't matter."

It was true, thought Louise. Everyone was smiling at her, as though she'd done something wonderful, instead of just interrupting the boring talk.

The tour guide swung the bus into a side street. "And here we have the Happy Days Motel, just as it was in Frog's day."

Someone laughed at that, as though the tour guide had made a joke.

"Hey, you mean Frog lived here? In Biscuit Creek? Someone who lived here actually became Prime Minister?"

"Of course," said the guide.

"I thought when you mentioned her before that she'd just visited here."

"This is what the tour is all about. We've come to see where Frog lived, where she spent her childhood."

"Hey, sweet! I never thought anyone famous came from Biscuit Creek."

The guide laughed. "You'd be surprised. Now, on your left we have The Dragon Chinese Restaurant. I'll just pause here for a moment so you can look down the main street from this angle. It's said that Frog's favourite take-away meal was sweet-and-sour chicken wings."

The man in the seat just behind leaned forward. "Can we go in and try some?" His accent was much thicker than the guide's.

The guide shook her head regretfully. "Normally, yes. But The Dragon isn't open on Saturday afternoons. This, of course, is the special tour—"

"Of course. Of course," said the man, sitting back in his seat. He laughed softy. "Just to have tried Frog's favourite food, from where she first tasted it perhaps..." He looked at his companion. "It would have been something special."

"I'm sorry," said the guide. "Of course, if you take the tour again another day it would be possible." She re-started the engine then changed gears, sort of clumsily, thought Louise. She didn't seem a very good driver for someone who did it every day.

"Note the gardens along here. Each of them is quite characteristic in its way. Biscuit Creek has a Garden Festival every October. There is no record, however, that Frog was ever interested in gardening."

Sensible girl, thought Louise.

"And now, we're nearing Biscuit Creek Central School, the school where Frog spent perhaps her most formative years. That's the oval coming up now and the basketball courts just above them. As far as we know, Frog rarely played basketball till she came to Biscuit Creek."

"She wasn't born here then?" asked Louise.

"No," said the guide. She didn't add anything more. She spoke to the bus at large again. "You can just see the domestic science block from here, it was completed only last year. And that's the library and the new auditorium." Another clash of gears and she edged the bus alongside the kerb opposite the front gates.

Louise stared at the school. It seemed more like a tatty brick blob than ever, with that sort of flat bare look that all schools get over the weekend.

Only one more day and she'd be there.

"Frog spent six years at this school," said the guide quietly. "It was here under the guidance of Mrs Prothero that she developed her first real interest in political science. Her early eloquent and passionate concern for developmental diversity is already evident in the one assignment of hers still held by the Biscuit Creek library, the one that already foreshadows that most famous of her speeches." The guide smiled. "I won't quote it. Like me you probably learnt that last paragraph off by heart at school."

"Each of us straddles the past and the future," someone murmured. "But some of us…" The voice stopped, as though the rest of the sentence was too well known to have to say.

The guide nodded, the crazy flaps on her hat bobbing. "Every time I hear it, though, every time I remember the words, it still moves me. If you'd all like to wander around and see the school first-hand for yourselves, we will meet back here at…" She glanced at her watch. "Three o'clock exactly."

The tourists stepped out of the bus. Some wandered across the road. Others stayed chatting on the footpath, glancing back at the bus, as though they were worried it might disappear, thought Louise, or as if it were more fascinating than the school beyond.

"Do you want to go and explore too?" asked the guide.

Louise shook her head. "No," she said. "It'll be bad enough on Monday with everyone there." The empty buildings looked like they were waiting to swallow passers-by.

The guide seemed to understand. "Would you like a sandwich?" she offered. "They're left over from lunch. We had a picnic down by the river. All part of the service."

Louise took a sandwich. It was baked beans and lettuce on white bread, her favourite. It seemed a funny sort of thing to give to adults at a picnic.

"Mum went to school here," she said, just for something to say. "I don't suppose it's changed much since then. It doesn't look like it has, anyway."

The guide took a sandwich too. "All things change, Nienza. It's only when you look back sometimes you realise how much. No one – no prophet, no fortune teller – has ever really predicted how much things will change. If you told your mother when she was a child how much things would change in her lifetime, she probably wouldn't have believed it. And if someone had told Frog the things that would have changed around her... Ah, well, maybe Frog might have believed. Frog was unique."

Louise took another baked-bean sandwich. "Why was she called Frog?"

The guide licked a stray baked bean off her fingers. "Oh, it's such a romantic story. Her husband called her Frog. This was long before they married, of course."

Louise giggled. "What sort of bloke would call someone he loved Frog?"

"They'd just met," the guide explained, "and she was wearing a cap like this." The guide touched the cap on her head. "That's why I wear it, of course, when I'm giving a tour. The cap was her trademark, if you like. She always wore it, had another made when the old one grew too shabby. And then some of her supporters took it up. Her husband had said, 'You look just like a frog,' or words to that effect, and the nickname stuck. I suppose she just made the best of it for a while and then she grew to like it. That was all anyone ever called her after a while, to the end of her life. Just Frog."

"She's dead then?"

"Yes, Nienza. She's dead. She's been dead for many years."

"Oh." Of course, she must be dead, thought Louise. Otherwise she'd have been in the news and then she would have heard of her. Even if you weren't interested in politics you couldn't ignore a name like "Frog".

It would have been good to have seen her on TV, Louise thought regretfully. Someone famous from Biscuit Creek.

"Do you give these tours all the time?" Louise hoped not. Mum was paid a percentage of the takings for everyone who came into the museum and for guiding historical tours through the town, too. It'd mean less money if a tour company gave them as well.

"Not often," said the guide. "This is a very special tour."

"How do you get to be a tour guide?"

"I did my... well, it's like a doctorate, a PhD, but not quite like that – on Frog and her political party. I have written articles about her too. You could really call me a specialist on Frog rather than a tour guide." The guide looked faintly amused.

"Oh," said Louise again.

Three of the tourists climbed back into the bus, though it wasn't nearly three yet. The others crossed the road too, as though they'd much rather be in the bus than explore the school.

Louise didn't blame them. Who'd want to look at Biscuit Creek School even if a famous Prime Minister did go there?

"What did Frog look like?" she asked finally.

"She was beautiful," said the tour guide. "Quite beautiful. Not a multistar — I mean, a movie star — sort of beauty. Her face was all wrong for that. But everyone who saw her spoke of how fascinating she was, how her face lit up when she was passionate about something. And Frog was passionate about many things. *What is the use of working for a cause if you don't live it heart and soul?* she used to say. *What's the point of living if you don't want things to change? You may as well be a grosrat in his hole...*"

"It would be nice to be beautiful," said Louise wistfully.

The guide patted her hand. "She wasn't always beautiful, Nienza. Like any truly beautiful person she grew into her beauty as she grew older."

"No," said the man behind. "She was always beautiful. Even when she was young she was beautiful, just in a different way." He smiled at Louise, strangely emphatic.

The tour guide smiled back. "Well, perhaps," she agreed. "Is everybody ready? Then we'll be off again. Next stop is the Blue Moon Café where Frog worked in the school holidays in her last two years of school. And, yes..." she said to the man behind Louise, "the café is open this afternoon. We can stop there, if you like. The specialty is Devonshire tea. Or coffee, if you'd prefer."

More giggles, though it wasn't really funny, thought Louise.

"And then the basketball courts. Frog's husband, Gavin, was an ardent basketball player all through school—"

"What did her husband do when he left school?" asked Louise, as the bus drew out from the kerb again. "Was he a politician too?"

"My, my word no. He was a microbiologist. 'He looks down and I look out,' Frog always said. She claimed they were a perfect combination. 'He keeps me grounded,' she said, 'whenever I'm tempted to fly away.' And over there is the Biscuit Creek Fire Station, the road up to the sewerage works, the ambulance depot..."

It was nearly five o'clock when the bus drew into the lane behind the museum again.

They'd had afternoon tea at the Blue Moon Café. (The tour guide had taken off her cap for that, to Louise's relief.)

They had driven past the cemetery, then up to the hill behind the town to admire the view and then past the old mill site.

FROG

Mum will be wondering where I am, thought Louise. *Not that anything much could happen to you in Biscuit Creek.*

The bus doors opened. Louise stepped down, then turned.

"Thank you," she said. "I really enjoyed it. It..." she hesitated. It had been good seeing the town with other strangers, but it was too embarrassing to try to explain.

The tour guide grinned. "It was a pleasure."

"A real pleasure," added the man in the seat behind, his voice deep and, like the guide's, strangely sincere.

The guide grinned suddenly. "Here," she said.

Before Louise realised what was happening, the guide had risen from her seat and plonked her bright-green cap on Louise's head.

"A souvenir," she said. "A gift from all of us."

The whole bus was grinning now.

No wonder, thought Louise. She must look like nothing on earth with the frog cap on her head.

"Thank you. I mean, not just for the cap, for the whole afternoon, for the tour, for everything. It sort of makes you look at Biscuit Creek differently knowing the Prime Minister of Australia once lived here."

The guide looked at her intently. "She wasn't Prime Minister of Australia," she said.

"But I thought you said—"

"She was the first Prime Minister of Mars." The bus doors shut. The engine revved and the bus drew down the lane.

Louise stood watching it, biting her lip. Adults! You think they're taking you seriously, then they come out with something like that – Prime Minister of Mars!

Maybe the whole day had just been a joke. Maybe there never had been anyone called Frog. Surely with a name like that she'd have remembered hearing something about her.

But the guide had seemed so sincere.

Louise was at the corner before she realised she still had the guide's dumb cap on her head. Maybe the cap was part of the joke too.

"Hey, frog head!"

Louise glanced up. Three boys wandered down the street opposite, the tallest balancing a basketball on one finger. He tossed it up and caught it.

"Hey, Frog!" he called again. "Where'd you get the hat?"

Louise grabbed the hat in embarrassment. She stumbled up the museum steps, then glanced down the road again. The boys were nearly at the corner now. The tall one turned again to look at her. His grin lit up his face.

Just my luck! thought Louise. On my first day here! I bet the name will stick now – just like it did to...

Louise dashed into the museum.

"Mrs Halibut! Mrs Halibut!"

"No, that property wasn't subdivided till the early 1900s; you're thinking of the other side of the family. What is it, Louise?" Mrs Halibut put down her tea cup. *They must have been sitting there talking for hours*, thought Louise.

"Mrs Halibut, I'm sorry, that kid out the window, do you know what his name is?"

Mrs Halibut crossed to the window just as the boys turned the corner.

"The one with dark hair and the basketball? That's Gavin Steadery. He's one of the Steadery boys from Wonga Hill — you remember Marcie Steadery, Jan?"

Louise realised her mouth was still open. She shut it, and stared out the window. The boys were halfway down the street now, but the tall one glanced back again at the museum.

"I remember her hair," said Louise's mother. "Bright red plaits and she never got them cut — she was the last girl in the class to have long hair. Louise, darling, where on earth did you get that hat? It looks like a… well, I don't know what it looks like."

Louise grinned. She shoved the cap back on her head. "Just call me Frog," she said.

WITCHES WHO MADE HISTORY

Maeve Friel

Illustrated by Nathan Reed

Witches Who Made History: Dame Walpurga of the Blessed Warts

By Jessica Diamond, Witch-in-Training

As you all know, witches once had iron teeth and ate small children for breakfast. So it was lucky for small children that it was easy to recognise a witch. They had hooked noses, tufts of hair sprouting from their ears and very very long chins. They smelled awful and flitted around the sky at night-time on old-fashioned broomsticks.

What you may not know is that they had to get *really* angry before they could fly off on their broom handles. Only a 100% humdinger of a hissy fit gave them the lift they needed to get off the ground. It was not only exhausting, it was dangerous because if they forgot, even for a split second, to stay in a bad temper, they tended to drop out of the sky like a stone and end up in the nearest duck-pond.

Nothing changed until Dame Walpurga of the Blessed Warts came along. We don't know much about Walpurga's early life although it goes without saying that she never got along with her sister witches. For one thing, she didn't care to eat small children for breakfast – or at any other time of day; and secondly, she was very jolly and sweet-tempered. Unfortunately, that meant that she could never get angry enough to fly.

Luckily, Dame Walpurga was a genius when it came to Spelling – so, one winter she made up a spell for each twig on her sweeping-brush. On the first day of spring, she cheerfully climbed up on to her roof, mounted her broom with the twigs facing her – and tweaked. What happened? Wey-hey – she took off!

The Dame had invented the Modern Witch's Right-Way-Up Broom!

It had twigs for Ignition, Ascending, Descending, Zooming and Reversing. It even had an Eject twig for ejecting unwelcome hangers-on like goblins or young dragons.

Soon, witches from north, south, east and west were dropping by to test-drive Walpurga's brooms. They all agreed that the Modern Broom was fabulous – at last, they could pop up on their brooms any time they liked and whizz off to a princess' christening or a coven meeting at the crossroads without having to get into a rage first. Flying without having to be mad was so easy and enjoyable. No longer did they risk falling out of the sky if they were distracted by a hunky-looking woodcutter or a gingerbread house. They formed their own flying club, the Broom Riders, and invented games like the Best

Zoom in a Room or Synchronised Ducking & Diving. Walpurga even built a twelve-seater Trambroom for witches who were too old to learn to fly the new brooms themselves and took them on excursions up on to the Milky Way. Witch life would never be the same again.

Sadly, Dame Walpurga's invention was not welcomed by the Powers-That-Be, the boss of Witches World Wide. Her name was Pluribella Strega, and I am very sorry to have to tell you that she was the grandmother of my teacher Miss Bella Strega. Pluribella was the kind of person who didn't like new things but, especially, she didn't like anyone else being more popular than her. She was always cross and liked to be the boss.

One night she hurtled off, spitting nails, from her home in the lost city of Hagopolis to Dame Walpurga's cottage. She stormed up the path, hurled the *New Brooms for Old* notice into

the well and screamed at Walpurga: "There is only ONE way to fly a broom."

She banned the Modern Broom!

But by now, witches had learned to love flying. They were not going to sit back and let the Powers-That-Be take away their new freedom. They met in secret underground places and muttered and grumbled until, at last, someone said:

"The Boss says we can't fly Dame Walpurga's Modern Broomstick but she never said anything about hot-air balloons."

"Or bath-mats."

"Or kites."

"Or bicycles with wings."

"All it would take is a bit of Spelling and a Charm or two."

Soon the skies were chock-a-block with witches flying everything from space-hoppers to garden forks. There were so many collisions and traffic jams and pile-ups that the other sky-users — flying horses, tooth fairies, dragons, angels on their clouds, Santa's reindeer — were furious. And you can't begin to imagine how cross the Powers-That-Be was.

She threw a massive wobbly and issued another decree.

"All Travelling is OUTLAWED. Flying,

on any class of broom, animal or machine is BANNED. Any witch found outside her own neighbourhood will be disenchantified." (Disenchantified means that she would be stripped of her witchy powers.)

Now everybody was unhappy because although the new Right-Way-Uppers were grounded so were the old-fashioned Wrong-Way-Uppers.

That was the beginning of the Broomstick Battles.

Walpurga's first task was to organise a way home under Cover of Darkness for any witch who had been stranded when the flying ban was introduced. (A Cover of Darkness is a very useful blanket that makes you invisible — if you would like one, my teacher Miss Strega sells them in her shop in the High Street for only three maravedis.)

Needless to say, there were spies everywhere, owls who couldn't help hooting to the Powers-that-Be, as well as bad fairies and evil goblins who switched road-signs. But within six months most of the Right-Way-Uppers had got home.

Then Walpurga hung loudspeakers on every tree and lamp-post offering the Wrong-Way-Uppers free Walpurga brooms to encourage them to join the Reclaim the Skies Movement. She and her supporters carried out daring midnight flights over Hagopolis, cackling happy flying songs at the Powers-That-Be while she squirted eye-of-newt and dragon-blood bombs back at them.

The Wrong-Way-Uppers fought too. There was a very brave group of ace pilots who called themselves The Besoms-R-Us Gang. They still liked their old-fashioned brooms but they didn't care for Pluribella's bossiness. Night after night, they zipped over Hagopolis, screeching down the chimney-pots at Pluribella and her cats.

As the Broomstick Battles raged, normal witch life almost came to a standstill. Cauldrons burned dry, cats and other familiars ran wild; spells were left uncast and everyone began to run out of basic brewing ingredients. You couldn't find a White Crow's Tail Feather or a Mandrake Root at any price. Moreover, Walpurga had no time to invent and the Powers-That-Be was too tired to be cross and bossy. Things fell apart. Everyone was sick of war. It was time to talk.

Judge Portia, an Italian witch (and incidentally the first judge to wear a wig made of cocker spaniel ears), locked Dame Walpurga and Pluribella in a room together. They were not allowed to leave until they saw sense. Finally, on 5th January of the witch year 380, they signed the Peace Agreement. The Broomstick Battles were over. Walpurga was declared the new Powers-That-Be. The Right-Way-Up Broom became the broom of choice for every modern witch.

But a curious thing happened after that.

Pluribella became quite sweet as soon as she lost her job.

"Frankly, my dear," she told me, "I was stuck up in Hagopolis for years with nothing but an attic full of smelly cats for company and the Bezoms-R-Us gang screeching down my chimney-pots night after night. I had had enough of being the Powers-That-Be. It's a terrible job. Walpurga is welcome to it."

And blinking cats and frisky bats, didn't Walpurga become very fierce when she became the boss. She even grew iron teeth and once threatened to gobble me up.

What was even stranger was that Pluribella and Walpurga went into business together and made a fortune selling bottled water from the well in Walpurga's cottage garden.

Needless to say, it was a runaway success.

The capital of Witches World Wide moved to Coven Garden, Dame Walpurga's old home, where it has remained to this day.

The cottage itself has long since disappeared – all that remains is one ivy-covered wall – but there is a statue of Dame Walpurga in the garden, seated on a three legged stool beside her well under a gnarled hawthorn tree.

It is one of the Seven Wonders of the Witch World, visited by more witches than any other witch attraction anywhere. Visitors hang little offerings on the hawthorn tree – tiny broomsticks, scraps of cape, wands, shoe buckles and scraps of paper covered with spells and incantations. They throw coins in the well for good luck and take home bottles of water to mix up their brews. Some witches like to rub the wart at the end of Walpurga's nose for good luck – it's like a shiny brass button now from all the fingers that have touched it.

Whether her blessed warts are magic, well, your guess is as good as mine but it is a fact that Dame Walpurga was one of the greatest witches in history. Without her invention of the Modern Broom, we would still be huffing and puffing and working ourselves into a terrible tizz just to get airborne. Even our noses and chins seem to be getting shorter since we stopped all that scowling. That means that we are less easy to recognise nowadays so be careful – those old-fashioned witches who like to eat young children for breakfast haven't all gone away, you know. They just look the same as you or me.

Neil Gaiman

IIOW TO SELL THE PONTI BRIDGE

My favourite Rogues' Club is the oldest and still the most exclusive in all the Seven Worlds. It was formed by a loose association of rogues, cheats, scoundrels and confidence men almost seventy thousand years ago. It has been copied many times in many places (there was one started quite recently, within the last five hundred years at any rate, in the City of London) but none of the other clubs matches the original Rogues' Club, in the city of Lost Carnadine, for atmosphere. No other club has quite so select a membership.

And the membership of the Lost Carnadine Rogues' Club is particularly select. You will understand the kind of person who makes it to membership if I tell you that I myself have seen, walking or sitting or eating or talking, in its many rooms, such notables as Daraxius Lo (who sold the Kzem a frogbat on a holy day), Prottle (who sold the palace of the King of Vandaria to the King of Vandaria) and the self-styled Lord Niff (who, I have heard it whispered, was the original inventor of the fox twist, the cheat that broke the bank at the Casino Grande). In addition, I have seen Rogues of inter-universal renown fail to gain admittance to even discuss their membership with the Secretary – on one memorable day I passed a famous financier, in company with the head of the Hy-Brasail mafia and a pre-eminent Prime Minister, on their way down the back stairs with the blackest of expressions upon their faces, having obviously been told not even to think about returning.

No, the ones who make it into the Rogues' Club are a high bunch. I am sure that you will have heard of each of them. Not under those names, of course, but the touch is distinctive, is it not?

I myself gained membership by means of a brilliant piece of creative scientific research, something that revolutionised the thinking of a whole generation. It was my disdain for regular methodology and, as I have said, creative research that gained me membership, and when I am in that part of the Cosmos I make a point of stopping off for an evening, taking in some sparkling conversation, drinking the club's fine wines and basking in the presence of my moral equals.

It was late in the evening and the log fire was burning low in the grate, and a handful of us sat and drank one of the fine dark wines of Spidireen in an alcove in the great hall. "Of course," one of my new friends was saying, "there are some scams that no self-respecting rogue would ever touch, they are so old and classless and tired. Like selling a tourist the Ponti Bridge."

"It's the same with Nelson's Column, or the Eiffel Tower, or the Brooklyn Bridge, back on my homeworld," I told them. "Sad little con-games, with as much class as a back-alley game of Find the Lady. But look on the good side. Nobody who ever sold the Ponti Bridge would ever get membership of a club like this."

"No?" said a quiet voice from the corner of the room. "How strange. I do believe it was the time I sold the Ponti Bridge that gained me membership of this club." A tall gentleman, quite bald and most exquisitely dressed, got up from the chair in which he had been sitting, and walked over to us. He was sipping the inside of an imported rhøm-fruit, and smiling, I think at the effect that he had created. He walked over to us, pulled up a cushion and sat down. "I don't believe we've met," he said.

My friends introduced themselves (the grey-haired deft-woman, Gloathis; the short, quiet dodger Redcap) as did I.

He smiled wider. "Your fame precedes each of you. I am honoured. You may call me Stoat."

"Stoat?" said Gloathis. "The only Stoat I ever heard of was the man who pulled the Derana Kite Job, but that was... what, over a hundred years ago. What am I thinking? You adopted the name as a tribute, I presume."

"You are a wise woman," said Stoat. "It would be impossible for me to be the same man." He leaned forward on his cushion. "You were talking about the sale of the Ponti Bridge?"

"Indeed we were."

"And you were all of the opinion that selling the Ponti Bridge is a measly scam, unworthy of a member of this club? And perhaps you are right. Let us examine the ingredients of a good scam. He ticked off the points on the fingers of his left hand as he spoke. "*Firstly* the scam must be credible. *Secondly* it must be simple, the more complex the more chance of error. *Thirdly,* when the sucker is stung he must be stung in such a way as to prevent him from ever turning to the law. *Fourthly*, the mainspring of any elegant con is human greed and human vanity. *Lastly,* it must involve trust – confidence, if you will."

"Surely," said Gloathis.

"So you are telling me that the sale of the Ponti Bridge – or any other major landmark not yours to sell – cannot have these characteristics? Gentlemen. Lady. Let me tell you my story.

"I had arrived in Ponti some years before almost penniless. I had but thirty gold crowns, and I needed a million. Why? I am afraid that is another story. I took stock of myself – I had the gold crowns and some smart robes. I was fluent in the aristocratic Ponti dialect, and I am, I pride myself, quite brilliant. Still, I could think of nothing that would bring me the kind of money I needed to have in the time by which I needed to have it. My mind, usually teeming and coruscating with fine schemes, was a perfect blank. So, trusting to my gods to bring me inspiration, I went on a guided tour of the city..."

Ponti lies to the South and to the East, a free city and port at the foot of the Mountains of Dawn. Ponti is a sprawling city, on either side of the Bay of Dawn, a beautiful natural harbour. Spaning the bay is the Bridge, which was built of jewels, of mortar and of magic, nearly two thousand years ago. There were jeers when it was first planned and begun, for none credited that a structure almost half a mile across could ever be successfully completed, or would stand for long once erected, but the Bridge was completed, and the jeers turned to gasps of awe and civic pride. It spanned the Bay of Dawn, a perfect structure that flashed and shone and glinted in myriad rainbow colours beneath the noon sun.

The tour guide paused at the foot of it. "As you can see, ladies and gentlemen, if you will examine closely, the Bridge is built entirely of precious stones – rubies, diamonds, sapphires, emeralds, chryolanths, carbuncles and such – and they are bound together with a transparent mortar which was crafted by the twin sages Hrolgar and Hrylthfgur out of a primal magic. The jewels are all real – make no mistake about that – and were gathered from all five corners of the world by Emmidus, King of Ponti at the time."

A small boy near the front of the group turned to his mother and announced loudly, "We did him in school. He's called Emmidus the Last, because there weren't any more after him. And they told us…"

The tour guide interrupted, smoothly. "The young man is quite correct. King Emmidus bankrupted the city-state obtaining the jewels, and thus set the scene for our current benificent Ruling enclave to appear."

The small boy's mother was now twisting his ear, which cheered the tour guide up immensely. "I'm sure you've heard that confidence-tricksters are always trying to play tourists for mugs by telling them that they are representing the Ruling Enclave, and that as the owners of the Bridge they are entitled to sell it. They get a hefty deposit, then scarper. To clarify matters," he said, as he said five times each day, and he and the tourists chuckled together, "the bridge is definitely not for sale." It was a good line. It always got a laugh.

His party started to make its way across the Bridge. Only the small boy noticed that one of their number had remained behind – a tall man, quite bald. He stood at the foot of the bridge, lost in contemplation. The boy wanted to point this out to everybody, but his ear hurt, and he said nothing.

The man at the foot of the bridge smiled abruptly. "Not for sale, eh?" he said, aloud. Then he turned and walked back to the city.

They were playing a game not unlike tennis with large heavy-strung racquets, and jewelled skulls for balls. The skulls were so *satisfying* in the way they *thunked* when hit cleanly, in the way they curved in great looping parabolas across the marble court. The skulls had never sat on human necks; they had been obtained, at great loss of life and significant expense, from a demon race in the highlands, and, afterwards, jewelled (emeralds and sweet rubies set in a lacy silver filigree in the eyesockets and about the jawbone) in Carthus's own workshops.

It was Carthus's serve.

He reached for the next skull in the pile and held it up to the light, marvelling at the craftsmanship, in the way that the jewels, when struck by the light at a certain angle, seemed to glow with an inner luminescence. He could have told you the exact value and the probable provenence of each jewel – perhaps the very mine from which it had been dug. The skulls were also beautiful: each formed of bone the colour of milky mother-of-pearl, translucent and fine. Each had cost him more than the value of the jewels set in its elegant bony face. The demon-race had now been hunted to the verge of extinction and the skulls were well-nigh irreplaceable.

He lobbed the skull over the net. Aathia struck it neatly back at him, forcing him to run to meet it (his footsteps echoing on the cold marble floor) and – *thunk* – hit it back to her.

She almost reached it in time. Almost, but not quite: the skull eluded her racquet and fell towards the stone floor and then, only an inch or so above the ground, it stopped, bobbing slightly, as if immersed in liquid, or a magnetic field.

It was magic, of course, and Carthus had paid most highly for it. He could afford to.

"My point, lady," he called, bowing low.

Aathia said nothing. Her eyes glinted like chips of ice, or like the jewels that were the only things she loved. Carthus and Aathia, jewel merchants. They made a strange pair.

There was a discreet cough from behind Carthus. He turned to see a white-tuniced slave holding a parchment scroll. "Yes?" said Carthus. He wiped the sweat from his face with the back of his hand.

"A message, Lord. The man who left it said that it was urgent."

Carthus grunted. "Who's it from?"

"I have not opened it. I was told it was for your eyes and the eyes of the Lady Aathia, and for no other."

Carthus stared at the parchment scroll but made no move to take it. He was a big man with a fleshy face, sandy receding hair and a worried expression. His business rivals — and there were many, for Ponti had become, over the years, the centre of the wholesale jewel business — had learned that his expression held no clue to his inner feelings. In many cases it had cost them money to learn this.

"Take the message, Carthus," said Aathia, and when he did not she walked around the net herself and plucked the scroll from the slave's fingers. "Leave us."

The slave's bare feet were soundless on the chill marble floor.

Aathia broke the seal with her sleeve-knife and unrolled the parchment. Her eyes flicked over it once, fast, then again at a slower pace. She whistled. "Here..." Carthus took it and read it through.

"I—I really don't know what to make of it," he said in a high, petulant voice. With his racquet he rubbed, absent-mindedly at the small criss-cross scar on his right cheek. The pendant that hung about his neck, proclaiming him one of the High Council of the Ponti Jewel Merchants' Guild, stuck, briefly, to his sweaty skin, and then swung free. "What do you think, my flower?"

"I am not your 'flower'."

"Of course not, lady."

"Better, Carthus. We'll make a real citizen of you yet. Well, for a start, the name is obviously false. 'Glew Croll' indeed! There are more men named Glew Croll in Ponti than there are diamonds in your storehouses. The address is obviously rented accommodation in the Undercliffs. There was no ring-mark on the wax seal. It's as if he has gone out of his way to maintain anonymity."

"Yes. I can see all that. But what about this 'business opportunity' he talks about? And if it is, as he implies, Ruling Enclave business, why would it be carried on with the secrecy he requests?"

She shrugged. "The Ruling Enclave has never been averse to secrecy. And, reading between the lines, it would appear that there is a great deal of wealth involved."

Carthus was silent. He reached down to the skull pile, leaned his racquet against it and placed the scroll beside it. He picked up a large skull. He caressed it gently with his blunt, stubby fingers. "You know," he said, as if speaking to the skull, "this could be my chance to get one up on the the rest of the bleeders on the Guild High Council. Dead-blood aristocratic half-wits."

"There speaks the son of a slave," said Aathia. "If it wasn't for my name you would never have made Council membership."

"Shut up." His expression was vaguely worried, which meant nothing at all. "I can show them. I'm going to show them. You'll see."

He hefted the skull in his right hand as if testing the weight of it, revelling in and computing the value of the bone, the jewels, the fine-worked silver. Then he spun round, suprisingly fast for one so big, and threw the skull with all his might at a far pillar, well beyond the field of play. It seemed to hang in the air for ever and then, with a painful slowness, it hit the pillar and smashed into a thousand fragments. The almost-musical tinkling sounds it made as it did so were very beautiful.

"I'll go and change and meet this Glew Croll then," muttered Carthus. He walked out of the room, carrying the scroll with him. Aathia stared at him as he left, then she clapped her hands, summoning a slave to clear up the mess.

The caves that honeycomb the rock on the north side of the Bay of Dawn, down into the bay, beneath the Bridge, are known as the Undercliffs. Carthus took his clothes off at the door, handing them to his slave, and walked down the narrow stone steps. His flesh gave an involuntary shiver as he entered the water (kept a little below blood-temperature in the aristocratic manner, but still chill after the heat of the day) and he swam down the corridor into an anteroom. Reflected light glimmered across the walls. On the water floated four other men and two women. They lounged on large wooden floats, elegantly carved into the shape of water-birds and fish.

Carthus swam over to an empty float – a dolphin – and hauled his bulk up on to it. Like the other six he wore nothing but the Jeweller's Guild High Council Pendant. All the High Council members, bar one, were there.

"Where's the President?" he asked of no one in particular.

A skeletal woman with flawless white skin pointed to one of the inner rooms. Then she yawned and twisted her body, a rippling twist, at the end of which she was off the float – hers was carved into the shape of a giant swan – and into the water. Carthus envied and hated her: that twist had been one of the twelve so-called "noble" dives. He knew that, despite having practised for years, he could not hope to emulate her.

"Effete cow," he muttered, beneath his breath. Still, it was reassuring to see other council members here. He wondered if any of them knew anything he didn't.

There was a splashing behind him, and he turned. Wommet, the Council President, was clutching Carthus's float. They bowed to each other, then Wommet (a small hunchback, whose ever-so-many-times-great-grandfather had made his fortune finding for King Emmidus the jewels that bankrupted Ponti, and had thus laid the foundations for the Ruling Enclave's 2,000-year rule) said, "He will speak to you next, Messire Carthus. Down the corridor on the left. It's the first room you come to."

The other council members, on their floats, looked at Carthus. They were aristocrats of Ponti, and they hid their envy and their irritation that Carthus was going in before them, although they did not hide it as well as they thought they did, and, somewhere deep inside, Carthus smiled.

He suppressed the urge to ask the hunchback what this business was all about, and he slipped off his float. The warmed seawater stung his eyes.

The room in which Grew Croll waited was up several rock steps, and was dry and dark and smoky. One lamp burned fitfully on the table in the centre of the room. There was a robe on the chair, and Carthus slipped it on. A man stood in the shadows beyond the lamp-light, but even in the murk Carthus could see that he was tall, and completely bald.

"I bid you good day," said a cultured voice.

"And on your house and kin also," responded Carthus.

"Sit down, sit down. As you have undoubtedly inferred from the message I sent you, this is Ruling Enclave business. Now, before another word is said, I must ask you to read and sign this oath of secrecy. Take all the time you need." He pushed a paper across the table: it was a comprehensive oath, pledging Carthus to silence about all matters discussed during their meeting on pain of the Ruling Enclave's "Extreme Displeasure" – a polite euphemism for death. Carthus read it over twice. "It... it isn't anything illegal is it?"

"Sir!" The cultured voice was offended. Carthus shrugged his great shoulders and signed. The paper was taken from his fingers and placed in a trunk at the far end of the hall. "Very good. We can get down to business then. Something to drink? Smoke? Inhale? No? Very well."

A pause.

"As you may have already surmised, Glew Croll is not my name. I am a junior administrative member of the Ruling Enclave." (Carthus grunted, his suspicions confirmed, and he scratched his ear.) "Messire Carthus, what do you know of the Bridge of Ponti?"

"Same as everyone. National landmark. Tourist attraction. Very impressive if you like that sort of thing. Built of jewels and magic. Jewels aren't all of the highest quality, although there's a rose diamond at the summit as big as a baby's fist, and reportedly flawless..."

"Very good. Have you heard the term 'magical half-life'?"

Carthus hadn't. Not that he could recall. "I've heard the term," he said, "but I'm not a magician, obviously, and..."

"A magical half-life, messire, is the nigromantic term for the length of time a magician, warlock, witch or whatever's magic lasts after his or her death. A simple hedge-witch's conjurations and so on will often vanish and be done with on the moment of her death. At the other end of the scale you have such phenomena as the Sea Serpent Sea, in which the purely magical sea-serpents still frolic and bask almost nine thousand years after the execution of Cilimwai Lah, their creator."

"Right. That. Yes, I knew that."

"Good. Then you will understand the import when I tell you that the half-life of the Ponti Bridge — according to the wisest of our Natural Philosophers — is little more than two thousand years. Soon, perhaps very soon Messire, it will begin to crumble and collapse."

The fat jeweller gasped. "But that's terrible. If the news got around…" He trailed off, weighing up the implications.

"Precisely. There would be panic. Trouble. Unrest. The news cannot be allowed to leak out until we are ready, hence this secrecy."

"I think I will have that drink now, please," said Carthus.

"Very wise." The bald nobleman unstoppered a crystal flagon and poured clear blue wine into a goblet. He passed it across the table and continued. "Any jeweller — and there are only seven in Ponti and perhaps two others elsewhere who could cope with the volume — who was permitted to demolish and keep the materials of the Ponti Bridge would regain whatever he paid for it in publicity alone, leaving aside the value of the jewels. It is my task to talk to the city's eight most prestigious wholesale jewellers about this matter.

"The Ruling Enclave has a number of concerns. As you can imagine, if the jewels were all released at once in Ponti, they would soon be almost worthless. In exchange for entire ownership of the bridge, the jeweller would have to undertake to build a structure beneath it, and as the bridge crumbles he or she would collect the jewels, and would undertake to sell no more than half a per cent of them within the city walls. You, as the senior partner in Carthus and Aathia, are one of the people I have appointed to discuss this matter with."

The jeweller shook his head. It seemed almost too good to be true – *if* he could get it. "Anything else?" he asked. His voice was casual. He sounded uninterested.

"I am but a humble servant of the Enclave," said the bald man. "They, for their part, will wish to make a profit on this. Each of you will submit a tender for the Bridge, via myself, to the Ruling Enclave. There is to be no conferring between you jewellers. The Enclave will choose the best offer and then, in open and formal session, the winner will be announced and then – and only then – will the winner pay any money into the city treasury. Most of the winning bid, as I understand things, will go towards the building of another bridge (out of significantly more mundane materials, I suspect) and to paying for a boat-ferry for the citizens while there is no Bridge."

"I see."

The tall man stared at Carthus. To the jeweller it seemed as if those hard eyes were boring into his soul. "You have exactly five days to submit your tender, Carthus. Let me warn you of two things. Firstly, if there is any indication of collaboration between any of you jewellers you will earn the Enclave's extreme displeasure. Secondly, if *anybody* finds out about the spell fatigue then we will not waste time in finding out which of you jewellers opened his mouth too widely and not too well. The High Council of the Ponti Jeweller's Guild will be replaced with another Council, and your businesses will be annexed by the City — perhaps to be offered as prizes in the next Autumn Games. Do I make my meaning plain?"

Carthus's voice was gravel in his throat. "Yes."

"Go then. Your tender in five days, remember. Send another in."

Carthus left the room as if in a dream, croaked "He wants you now," to the nearest High Council member in the anteroom and was relieved to find himself outside, in the sunlight and the fresh air. Far above him the jewelled heights of the Ponti Bridge stood, as they had stood, glinting and twinkling and shining down on the town, for the last two thousand years.

He squinted: was it his imagination, or were the jewels less bright, the structure less permanent, the whole glorious bridge subtly less magnificent than before? Was the air of permanence that hung about the bridge beginning to fade away?

Carthus began to calculate the value of the bridge in terms of jewel-weight and volume. He wondered how Aathia would treat him if he presented her with the rose-diamond from the summit; and the High Council would not view him as a *nouveau riche* upstart, not him, not if he was the man who bought the Ponti Bridge.

Oh, they would all treat him better. There was no doubt of that.

One by one, the man who called himself Glew Croll saw the jewel merchants. Each reacted in his or her own way – shock or laughter, sorrow or gloom – at the news of the spell-fatigue in the binding of the Ponti Bridge. And, beneath the sneers or the dismay, each of them began to judge profits and balance sheets, mentally judge and guess possible tenders, activate spies in rival jewellers' houses.

Carthus himself told no one anything, not even his beloved, unattainable Aathia. He locked himself in his study and wrote tenders, tore them up, wrote tenders once again. The rest of the jewellers were similarly occupied.

The fire had burned out in the Rogues' Club, leaving only a few red embers in a bed of grey ash, and dawn was painting the sky silver. Gloathis, Redcap and I had listened to the man called Stoat all night. It was at this point in his narrative that he leaned back on his cushion, and he grinned.

"So there you have it, friends," he said. "A perfect scam. Eh?"

I glanced at Gloathis and Redcap, and was relieved to see that they looked as blank as I felt.

"I'm sorry," said Redcap. "I just don't see..."

"You don't see, eh? And what about you, Gloathis? Do you see? Or are your eyes covered with mud?"

Gloathis looked serious. She said, "Well... you obviously convinced them all that you were a representative of the Ruling Enclave – and having them all meet in the anteroom was an inspired idea. But I fail to see the profit in this for you. You've said that you need a million, but none of them is going to pay anything to you. They are waiting for a public announcement that will never come, and then the chance to pay their money into the public treasury..."

"You think like a mug," said Stoat. He looked at me and raised an eyebrow. I shook my head. "And you call yourself rogues."

Redcap looked exasperated. "I just don't see the profit in it! You've spent your thirty gold coins on renting the offices and sending the messages. You've told them you're working for the Enclave, and they will pay everything to the Enclave..."

It was hearing Redcap spell it out that did for me. I saw it all and I understood, and as I understood I could feel the laughter welling up inside me. I tried to keep it inside, and the effort almost choked me. "Oh, priceless, priceless," was all I could say for some moments. My friends stared at me, irritated. Stoat said nothing, but he waited.

I got up, leaned in to Stoat and whispered in his ear. He nodded, once, and I began to chortle once again.

"At least one of you has some potential," said Stoat. Then he stood up. He drew his robes around him, and swept off down the torch-lined corridors of the Lost Carnadine Rogues' Club, vanishing into the shadows. I stared after him as he left. The other two were staring at me.

"I don't understand," said Redcap.

"What did he do?" begged Gloathis.

"Call yourself rogues?" I asked. "I worked it out for myself. Why can't you two simply... Oh, very well. After the jewellers left his office he let them stew for a few days, letting the tension build and build. Then, secretly, he arranged to see each of the jewellers at different times and in different places – probably low-life taverns.

"And in each tavern he would greet the jeweller and point out the one thing that he – or they – had overlooked. The tenders would be submitted to the Enclave through my friend. He could arrange for the jeweller he was talking to – Carthus, say – to put in the winning tender.

"For of course, he *was* open to bribery."

Gloathis slapped her forehead. "I'm such an oaf! I should have seen it! He could easily have raked in a million gold coins' worth of bribes from that lot. And once the last jeweller paid him, he'd vanish. The jewellers couldn't complain – if the Enclave thought they'd tried to bribe someone they thought to be an Enclave official, they'd be lucky to keep their right arms, let alone their lives and businesses. What a perfect con."

And there was silence in the Hall of the Lost Carnadine Rogues' Club. We were lost in contemplation of the brilliance of the man who sold the Ponti Bridge.

MORE BITS OF AN AUTOBIOGRAPHY I MAY NOT WRITE

Morris Gleitzman

I'll never forget when we got our first dog. The excitement! The noise! The joyful howls (the dog). The puddles on the carpet (me).

I'd read all the books and knew exactly what to do. First, give her a feed.

"Better let us do that, Dad," said the kids, taking the bowl. "Better safe than sorry."

I was indignant. The dog was indignant.

"Why?" I demanded.

"Because," whispered the kids so the dog wouldn't hear, "you're hopeless with pets."

I was deeply hurt. "That goldfish," I retorted, "died of a bad cold."

The kids looked at me sternly. "It died," they said, "because of what you fed it."

I was even more indignant. "The box had pictures of fish on it," I said. "How was I to know it was cat food?"

The kids looked sad. The dog looked nervous. I took her for a walk round the block.

"We'll do that," called the kids, running to catch up. "Better safe than sorry."

I boiled with indignation. The dog tried to hand them the lead.

"You're not being fair," I said. "I've never had a single accident taking a dog for a walk round the block. Or a fruit-bat. Or a blue-tongue lizard."

"That's right," said the kids sadly. "Just a mouse. What on earth possessed you to throw that stick and tell our mouse to fetch it? With a hungry cat on the loose whose dinner you'd just fed to the goldfish?"

Before I could answer, I realised I was holding an empty lead. The dog had disappeared.

We found her halfway up a lamppost, trembling with fear. The kids managed to coax her down, but only after I'd come to an agreement with them. If anything happened to the dog, they'd have me arrested.

So I enrolled us both in training and obedience classes. The dog graduated after a month, but I needed an extra six weeks.

*

It was a very bright jumper.

"Absolutely you, sir," said the menswear assistant, putting on sunglasses.

I squinted at my reflection. I looked like I'd just staggered out of an explosion in a paint factory.

"You know how computer screens have millions of colours?" continued the assistant. "Well this jumper's got even more millions. It does suit you, sir. The greens match your complexion."

I wore it home. Cars swerved, buses ran into each other, and a light plane made a forced landing dragged down by the temporarily blinded birds clinging to its wings.

At my place people and animals dived for cover.

"Dad," winced the kids, shielding their eyes with thick metal baking trays. "Take it off. All the neighbours are pulling their curtains."

Patiently I explained how I was going to speak about my books at a school the next day and how I was terrified the students would lose interest and start talking among themselves.

"Bright colours grab people's attention," I said. "Look at Elton John, and fire engines."

"Dad," sighed the kids, shielding the goldfishes' eyes with lolly wrappers. "If the audience cops an eyeful of that jumper they may never be able to read another word you write."

"Rubbish," I said. "My readers are tough, specially round the eyeballs."

I was right. At the school the next day I had everyone's attention from the moment I walked in. I told them all about my latest book – the characters, the themes, where they could buy it and how I'd come round and clean their car if they did. Even after I'd finished speaking I could see every pair of eyes in the room still on me.

Well, not exactly on me. More on my jumper. Then I noticed every pair of lips in the room was moving and every voice was murmuring something.

"Two million six hundred and forty-two thousand nine hundred and twenty-seven," they were saying. "Two million six hundred and forty-two thousand nine hundred and twenty-eight..."

*

Bushfire!

Tummies go wobbly at the thought. One time ours almost jumped into jelly bowls and hid in the fridge. Walls of flame, two kilometres long and a hundred metres high, roaring towards our suburb at ninety kilometres an hour!

At our place we knew the emergency drill:

1. Move to Alaska.
2. If there's not enough time for that, pack one small bag each and wait to be evacuated.

The kids were packed in minutes. "Dad," they yelled, "get a move on! A few essential items into a bag! Quickly!"

"I'm doing it as fast as I can," I protested. "This zip won't close."

The kids looked at my bulging bag.

"Dad," they said, "take the television out."

Outside, the sky was dark with smoke. The wind flung ash against the windows. We could feel the air inside the house heating up.

The kids gave a cry of alarm. A pink liquid was dripping from the bottom of my bag.

"Oh no," they shouted. "The wax seals on the important family documents are melting!"

"Relax," I said. "It's just raspberry ripple ice-cream."

The kids gave me a look almost as scorching as the flames four kilometres to the north.

"You said essential items," I protested.

"Essential items," they replied, "means birth certificates, insurance papers, passports, important letters and family photos."

"And Garfield slippers?" I added hopefully.

Just then the wind changed and our suburb was saved. Within a few days the only things still burning at our place were my cheeks. OK, the raspberry ripple ice-cream had been a silly choice. With only minutes to salvage my most precious possessions, I'd panicked. Next time I'd do it differently. Next time I'd pause, breathe deeply, think straight, and take the choc chip.

*

The kids were firm but fair.

"We want you to promise," they said, "to look after our polluted planet and its scarce resources and not make any more unnecessary trips in the car."

I promised.

They opened the boot and let me out.

"Because let's face it, Dad," they said when we'd got to our destination. "You are pretty lazy when it comes to walking."

I couldn't deny it so I concentrated on trying to find a parking space. Which isn't easy in a shop.

From that day, though, I did try to keep my promise. When I needed milk, or a newspaper, or socks, instead of driving I walked. And I had to admit it wasn't so bad. In fact it made getting the socks much easier because my wardrobe is quite close to the bed and it had always been a bit of a squeeze getting the car into the bedroom.

I started doing my supermarket shopping entirely on foot. (Except for one time when I was overcome with exhaustion between Frozen Foods and Breakfast Cereals and had to hitch a ride on someone's trolley.)

When I went to the cinema I left the car behind completely (not just at the ticket desk).

I went to the dentist on foot. (Well, part of the way. The kids had to carry me the last fifty metres, as usual.)

I even went to the carwash on foot. (Not such a good idea. Those rotating plastic brushes really scratch your scalp.)

I went everywhere on foot for several weeks and the kids were very proud of me. I walked down the hall to their room and they told me themselves.

I wished I could feel proud too. But I couldn't, because I knew the real reason why I wasn't making any more unnecessary trips in the car — I couldn't remember which shop I'd parked it in.

*

It was my first time and I was determined to do a good job. I took a deep breath and spoke clearly into the microphone.

"Good morning, ladies and gentlemen," I said. "I would like to demonstrate the safety features of this Boeing 767."

The kids looked up from their cornflakes and rolled their eyes.

"Dad," they said. "It's not a Boeing 767, it's a house."

Typical. Here I was, trying to keep them safe and healthy, and all they could do was criticise.

"If you require oxygen," I continued, "a mask will fall from the kitchen cupboard above your heads. Place it firmly over your nose and mouth and breathe normally, but watch you don't suck in any teaspoons."

"Dad," said the kids, "look out the window. Those white blobs aren't clouds, they're Mrs Bryant's poodles. We're not thirty-six thousand feet up, we're at home."

"Exactly," I said. "Eighty-seven percent of all accidents happen at home, and only zero point zero zero zero three per cent happen on planes. Why? Because on planes they take safety seriously. In case of emergency, your life jackets are located under your dining chairs."

I watched as the kids stopped straining against their seat belts trying to reach the milk, and thought about this.

"Gee," they said, brows furrowed, "you've got a point."

I gave a small triumphant smile as I pointed to the nearest exits. My plan was a success.

The Boeing 767 arrived a week later.

"Your kids ordered it," said the second-hand plane dealer. "But they said you'd pay. That's eighty million dollars, plus two million for delivery and mudflaps."

I stood there, mouth open. The bowl of cornflakes I'd been eating slipped from my fingers and nearly fell on my foot.

"By the way," said the dealer. "I wouldn't leave it there blocking the street like that, it might cause an accident."

I ignored him. He was just trying to sell me a hanger.

*

I don't know about you, but I've never been very good at watching TV while I'm being stared at. Specially by a dog with a lead in its mouth and two kids with cricket bats in theirs.

"Dad," said the kids, "you promised you'd take us to the park."

"Wmpf," agreed the dog.

"Don't talk with your mouths full," I said, but they were right, I had promised. "We agreed we'd go," I reminded them, "after I've finished watching *The Bill*."

"But Dad," they wailed, "we thought you meant one episode on air, not two hundred and eighty-seven episodes on DVD."

I sighed.

"Please," I said, "I'm trying to concentrate."

I turned back to episode fifteen. Or was it sixteen? This was criminal.

"We'll go after I've finished watching *The Bill*," I said firmly, "and nothing you can say will make me change my mind."

"Suit yourself," said the kids, "but if you don't get any exercise, you'll die."

The park was cold and wet, but I didn't care because I took a brilliant diving catch.

"Howzat!" I yelled triumphantly through the mud.

The umpire shook his head.

"Wmpf," he said, licking his bottom.

On the way home I decided there must be a way to combine telly and exercise and mud-free nostrils. That night I experimented.

"Who wants a Malteser?" I asked, tossing one up and swinging my table-tennis bat.

It was a big success with the kids. They quickly learned that when we had a TV dinner and there was no food on the plates, they had to leave their mouths open because I'd be chipping the peas in with a golf club and whacking the rissoles in with a squash racquet.

The dog liked it too. A few nights later, when I sliced my shot with the billiard cue and put his can of dog food through the TV screen in the middle of episode ninety-three of *The Bill*, I was sure he smiled.

THE DAY EVERYTHING EXPLODED

Andy Griffiths and Terry Denton

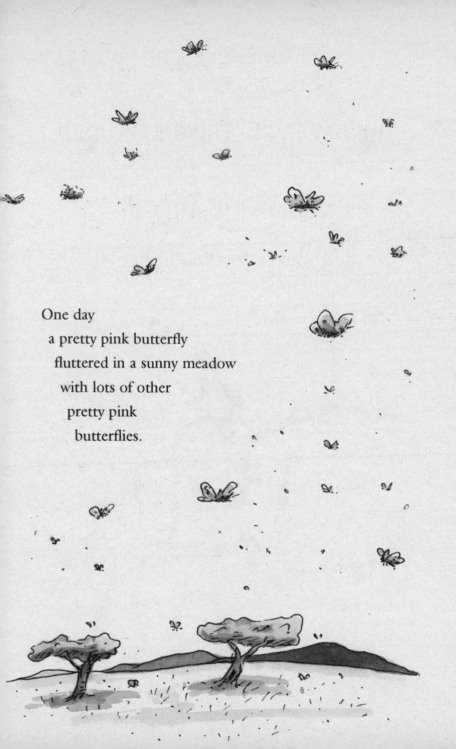

One day
  a pretty pink butterfly
  fluttered in a sunny meadow
  with lots of other
  pretty pink
  butterflies.

A beautiful little bluebird sang

sweetly in the willow tree.

Fluffy white lambs frollicked

in the soft green grass.

Then,
all of a sudden,

the pretty pink butterfly exploded.

Then another pretty pink
butterfly exploded.

Then all the pretty pink
butterflies exploded.

The blue bird exploded.

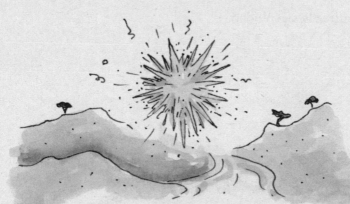

The willow tree exploded.

The fluffy white lambs stopped frolicking . . .

and
exploded.

The soft
green grass
exploded.

The meadow exploded.

A man walking past the
meadow exploded.

The man's wife exploded.

Every living creature on Earth
exploded.

Then everything else,
including the Earth,
exploded.

The moon
and
the planets
and
the sun exploded.

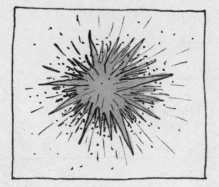

The galaxy exploded.

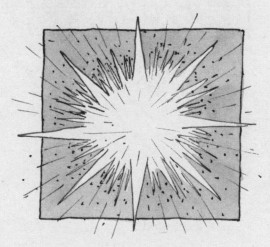

The universe exploded.

Then the explosion
exploded.

Then the explosion
of the explosion
exploded.

Then the explosion
of the explosion
of the explosion
exploded.

And
that was
the end
because
there
was
nothing
left
to
explode

. . . not
even
a pretty
pink
butterfly.

THE END

RTI

Anthony Horowitz

This is a chapter that I meant to write for Stormbreaker, *the first Alex Rider book. I somehow left it out, so I've written it for* Midnight Feast.

Alex Rider is a fourteen-year-old schoolboy being trained as a spy. He has been given a code name — Cub — and sent for training with the SAS in Wales. The other men in his patrol are Wolf, Eagle, Snake and Fox. All of them, and in particular Wolf, resent having a boy in a man's world and the training period has been bitter and tough...

Alex woke suddenly, brutally, wrenched out of his sleep. He was aware of hands, pulling away the covers. A face in a black balaclava mask. Two pitiless eyes gazing at him as if he were an exhibit in a museum. He opened his mouth to speak, but before he could say a word, he was jerked out of bed and into the night. It was cold outside, with a light drizzle hanging in the air. Alex was dressed only in shorts and a T-shirt. He shivered, wondering what the hell was going on.

The SAS training camp had been taken over while he slept, exhausted by the exercises of the day before. There were vehicles parked all around him, lights, men moving in and out of the shadows, the crackle of a distant radio. Alex wondered briefly what had happened to the men in his squadron but then decided he was actually much more concerned about what was going to happen to him. Two men had taken hold of him. His arms were clamped between them. He was half-carried across the yard, his feet dragging in the mud behind him. If he had been a sack of potatoes, they wouldn't have treated him less gently.

They took him into a half-derelict barn on the other side of the camp. The SAS had been based in what had once been a farm, and Alex guessed that this building might have been used to store feed. It still had an earthy, slightly sour smell. But there was nothing in there now apart from a chair, a naked light bulb and a hard cement floor. Moisture trickled down the rough brick walls. Alex was slammed into the chair and pinned in place. Another man appeared from nowhere. So now there were three of them, all dressed in battle fatigues and balaclavas. They surrounded him.

"Your name," one of them demanded.

"It's Cub," Alex replied.

"Your real name."

"I can't give you that…"

"What are you doing with the SAS? You're a bloody schoolboy! Why are you here?"

"I'm not allowed to tell you…"

A face closed in on him. Alex had never seen such ugly eyes. The mouth twisted behind the stocking mask. "You can tell us!" it sneered. "I'm giving you permission."

"My name is Cub," Alex repeated. It was the code name he had been given when he first arrived. None of the men in the SAS used their true identities. The eyes narrowed. Alex could see the anger and the cruelty they contained. They belonged to a man who hadn't expected to be defied – and certainly not by a teenager.

"You will tell us," he snarled. "Trust me on that. You'll tell us everything we want to know before this night is over."

A signal must have been given. Alex was pulled off the chair and manhandled out of the room, his toes scraping against the concrete. He was fully awake now, and his eyes had got used to the dark so he was able to make out more details of what was happening in the camp. They had been invaded. It was as simple as that. The men were all soldiers – obviously English. But they were the enemy. Who had sent them? What exactly did they want? There were three trucks parked to one side and – beyond them – an awkward-looking vehicle that looked like a caravan except that it was perched high up on six thick rubber wheels. More soldiers were moving between the buildings. As he was taken across the yard, he saw Wolf being dragged the other way. The SAS man was no friend of his. In fact, nobody had tried harder to make him feel unwelcome. But now, for a brief second, their eyes met. Alex was astonished to see that Wolf was looking scared. The invaders carried Alex over to one of the other farm buildings and threw him inside. There was a metal door, which slammed shut behind him. He had landed on the floor, and he picked himself up slowly. That was when he saw that he wasn't alone.

The three other members of his unit – Snake, Fox and Eagle – were sitting slumped on wooden benches. Like him, they were dressed only in their night clothes and he guessed they had also been rudely woken and pulled out of bed. Fox, the youngest of the three, had been hurt. There was a trickle of blood coming out of the corner of his mouth. His fair hair was damp and untidy. The other two men seemed to be deep in thought. Nobody was saying anything.

"What's happening?" Alex asked.

There was no answer. Alex felt a spurt of annoyance. None of the men in the unit ever spoke to him. He had begun to get used to it. But this was different. For once they were all in the same boat – and it seemed to be sinking fast.

"Tell me what's going on!" Alex demanded.

Fox glanced at Eagle, who nodded slowly. "RTI," he said, and spat.

"RTI?"

"RTI training. Resistance to Interrogation."

Eagle took over. "They're testing our ability to keep quiet if we're captured by the enemy," he explained. "We tell them anything except our code names, we're binned. We're out of the SAS!"

"Who are they?" Alex asked.

"Green Jackets." This time it was Snake who answered. "A local unit. They hate our guts – because they know we're the best. So they really enjoy this."

Alex's head swam. British soldiers attacking British soldiers… and it was all just another training exercise! Not for the first time, he wondered how he had managed to get caught up in all this.

"We talk, we get thrown out," Snake continued. "And that's exactly what they want."

"But it's just an exercise," Alex said. "They can't hurt us."

Fox smiled and Alex saw the blood on his teeth. "You think I just slipped?" he asked.

"They can do what they like," Snake said. "One of us winds up in hospital, they can say it was just an accident."

"And accidents do happen!" Eagle spat in disgust.

Ten minutes later, the door opened again and Wolf was thrown in. He landed flat on his stomach, and Alex saw that his head and the upper part of his body were soaking wet. There was a bruise on the side of his cheek. "The pigs!" rasped Wolf. He lay where he was, his shoulders heaving. "The lousy, stinking..." Slowly, he pulled himself off the floor. "They laid into me!" he exclaimed, and Alex could hear the surprise in his voice. "They were really enjoying themselves!"

"Did you tell them anything?" Eagle asked.

"Of course not." Wolf's eyes settled on Alex. "What about you, Cub? I bet you told them. I bet you blabbed."

"No, I didn't." Alex was angry now. Wolf had picked on him from the day he'd arrived. He had never trusted him, never even given him a chance.

"But you will... and you might as well know now. If you blow it, we all blow it. Because we're a unit. It only takes one of us to talk and we'll all be out of here."

"So what happens now?" Alex asked.

"They let us sweat it out," Fox said. "It might be an hour. It might be a few minutes. But one thing you can be sure about. They'll come for us again..."

Alex ignored him. He went over to the door and examined it. The door was a solid metal sheet, fitting into a metal frame, bolted from the outside. The room itself had once been used for dipping sheep. There were a few shelves, rotten now, with some rusting canisters that might once have contained chemicals. A single barred window looked out on to the night. He glanced at it briefly, but it was obvious he wasn't going to get out that way. He examined the floor. It was made up of heavy paving slabs, but in the middle there was a trench – square, and about half a metre deep, lined with concrete. There was a circular metal plate at the far end. It reminded Alex of an oversized bath plug. Then he realised what it was. A manhole cover.

"What's this?" Alex demanded.

Wolf ignored him. But Fox slowly turned his head.

"There's some sort of drain," Alex said. "Can you help me get the cover off?"

Wolf scowled. "You really think they'd bung us in here if there was a drain big enough for us to crawl out?" he asked.

Alex examined the cover. Wolf was right. It was barely even the size of a dustbin lid. But even so… "You're adults," he said simply.

Fox saw what he was thinking. The Green Jackets would have used this place before. But only for fully-grown men. Alex was half their size – slim for his age. Wolf still didn't move, but Fox and Eagle came over to the trench. Somehow, they managed to get their fingers under the heavy lid. They prised it off to reveal a narrow tunnel, running out of the room, underneath the wall. Alex looked down, already wishing he hadn't suggested this. The tunnel was pitch-black and slimy from recent rain. It might run a hundred metres before it surfaced. It might not surface at all.

"You think you can get through that?" Fox asked.

Alex nodded, not trusting himself to speak.

"Here!" Snake had produced a small torch. He flicked it on. "You're lucky. I always sleep with this in my pocket."

"Yeah," Alex nodded. "This really is my lucky night."

He knelt down beside the opening. He could already smell the chemicals rising up out of the mud. He wondered how long it had been since the sheep dip had last been used. Could he really do this? For a moment, he doubted himself. Then Wolf spoke. "Good luck," he said. They were the first two words he had ever addressed to Alex that weren't a jibe or an insult. That decided him. Alex wriggled forwards on his stomach and entered the tunnel.

It was pitch-black. But for Snake's torch, he wouldn't have had the courage even to begin. Alex was squeezing himself into a circular opening that was hardly bigger than his shoulders. He knew that he was only a few metres underground, but even so, he felt as if he was buried alive and had to force himself to breathe evenly, not to panic. The floor of the tunnel was wet and slippery… at least that helped him a little, making it easier for him to slide himself along. But the stink of ancient chemicals made him sick. The torch was clamped between his teeth and he could feel the bile rising in his throat. He wanted to scream. He wished he had never volunteered. He willed himself on. The beam of the torch showed that the tunnel continued straight, then came to a sudden halt. A nasty thought suddenly sprang into Alex's mind. If he came to a dead end, would he be able to manoeuvre himself backwards again? At least Snake and the others knew he was there. If he didn't reappear soon, they would raise the alarm. And hopefully someone would reach him before he passed out and suffocated in the cold slime and the darkness.

He came to the end and twisted his head round, trying to look up. It seemed that the roof was solid. Somehow he managed to get his hand above his head and felt a hard metal surface. A second manhole cover? He pushed. Nothing happened. Alex swore silently through gritted teeth. He had come all this way for nothing. The exit was sealed. But then he remembered Fox and Eagle, prising off the first lid. It had been heavy, even for two men. He put his hand flat against the metal and pushed again. This time there was a little movement. He pressed upwards with all his strength and was rewarded by a grating sound as the second manhole cover came free. Delicious night air flooded in through a crack and he saw the glimmer of moonlight. He dropped the torch, letting it disappear into the darkness. If there was anyone up there on the surface, he didn't want to advertise that he was on the way. Using both hands now, he slid the cover far enough back to create a crescent-shaped doorway to freedom. He waited a few seconds, listening out for the sound of approaching footsteps, then pulled himself through. His head came up in the middle of the courtyard. There was nobody in sight.

Filthy and gasping, Alex emerged into the night air, then squatted down, searching for any sign of movement. He was still dressed only in the T-shirt and shorts. The material was soaked through. Dark green slime oozed down his legs. He caught his breath. He must look like a nightmare! The creature from the black lagoon...

He took his bearings. The building where the SAS men were being held was right in front of him, but he could see at once that getting them out wouldn't be as easy as he'd hoped. The door wasn't just bolted. There was a big padlock on it – and even if Alex managed to break it open, he'd make too much noise. They'd all be captured again before they had time to move.

The half-ruined barn where he had been interrogated was on the other side, some distance away. It seemed to be empty, but at the moment there was nobody left to interrogate. Now his attention was drawn to the vehicle that he had noticed when he'd been dragged over to the cell. It was parked on a slope, about twenty metres away: a rectangular green box perched high up on thick rubber wheels. It had reminded him before of a caravan. Certainly it had windows. And there were lights coming from inside. But looking at it again, he saw that it was more like a Portakabin or even a tank. It was an ugly thing. Only the army could have dreamed up something like it.

In fact the vehicle was an S-250 GRASS shelter, standard army issue. The GRASS stood for Gichner Relocatable Accommodations Shelter System and it was being used as a temporary base by the men who had grabbed Alex and his unit. On an impulse he hurried over to it, crouching low, still afraid of being seen. But for the moment he was safe. The men inside were too high up. Even if they had chanced to glance out of the windows, they would have looked across the courtyard, well above his head. One of the windows was open. He heard voices coming from inside.

"Let's get back to them, then!"

"Finish your tea. We've got all night." Alex recognised the second voice. It belonged to the man who had threatened him.

"I'm really going to enjoy this..."

"Let's use the bath," a third voice said. "Fill it up with freezing water and try half-drowning them."

"What about the kid?" This was the first voice again. "I say we start with the kid. He'll be easy to break."

"Yeah… break his neck!" someone said, and they all laughed.

Alex knew he didn't have much time. He quickly examined the GRASS shelter, the fat tyres, resting on chocks. The brake lever at the back…

The idea came to him instantly. Getting the chocks out was easier than he had thought it would be, but there was a complicated lock system on the brake which took him a few precious moments to work out. A lever with a button, a pin holding everything in place. He slid the pin out, but the button was so stiff that he had to use both hands, and all his strength, to force it down. There was a loud click. He had released the lever and he gently lowered it. The brake was off – but the GRASS shelter didn't move. Alex rested a shoulder against the back and pushed. He was lucky. The soldiers must have parked in a hurry. The slope was fairly steep. It took only a little effort and the wheels began to turn.

There were six Green Jackets inside the shelter. Snake had been right about them. Three of them had once been rejected by the SAS and so they hated anyone who had been allowed to join. The other three just hated everyone. All of them had been happy to volunteer for RTI training. In fact, every year there was quite a queue to see who would get the privilege. Now, one of them looked out of the window. "Boss..." he muttered.

The man he was talking to was huge with a shaven head, small eyes and two gold-capped teeth. "What is it?" he demanded.

"Are we moving?" the first man asked.

The GRASS shelter was indeed moving. It was already rolling down the hill and it was picking up speed all the time. As Alex watched, it bounced through the long grass and smashed into a hedge. There was the sound of branches scratching against metal – but there was no way the hedge could hold back anything so big. It continued through and – moving faster than ever – disappeared into the night.

Inside the shelter, the Green Jackets were scrambling for the door. Hot tea was splashing all around them. Mugs had rolled off the table and smashed. Magazines and briefing documents were scattering. The shaven-headed man managed to grab on to the handle...

... just as the GRASS shelter catapulted off the edge of a cliff.

The SAS camp was in the Brecon Beacons. Mountains and cliffs had all played their part in the training. In a way, the Green Jackets were lucky. They were only a hundred and fifty metres up in the air and there was a lake – ice-cold and black – waiting to break their fall. The result of Alex's work would be two broken legs, a broken collarbone, eleven cracked ribs and a severe concussion. But nobody would actually be killed.

Meanwhile, Alex had already turned his attention to the dipping shed. He found a piece of metal and used it to snap open the padlock, then dropped it and opened the door. Wolf was the first out. He took a look round the deserted farm. Then he turned his eyes back to Alex.

"Where is everyone?" he demanded.

Alex shrugged. "I think they've sloped off," he said.

A MIDNIGHT FEAST

Brian Jacques

Dear Diary...

Let me tell you about last night's party. Talk about stress and upset! That's the last Midnight Feast I'm putting on mate!

Oh, and another thing: I'm finished with that lot from Once Upon a Time Storybook Land. Never again. In fact, never never land again!

Anyhow, the clock had struck twelve as we all sat down. I smiled to myself as I watched the dear little mouse running up it. Suddenly... woffo! A cat wearing a pair of outsized wellies dived on the mouse and scoffed it! Not only that but the cat knocked my clock over, and smashed it to bits: casing, chimes, glass, everything. Serves me right I suppose, it was my Grandfather clock and was too tall for the shelf. So puddenheaded me put it on the floor.

Honestly, he's nothing but trouble that Puss in Boots. Last I saw of him he'd got into a fight with a lion and a unicorn, battling all over the High Street. I hope the cops lock them all up. Hooligans!

But back to my Midnight Feast. That old woman who lives in a shoe, hah, she whacked little Jack Horner for sticking his thumb in a pie. Nobody seemed to blame her really, he was sticking his thumb in pies left right and centre, crying out "what a good boy am I!"

Disgusting little prig. Most unhygienic.

By the way, don't ever serve pies at a Midnight Feast. They're nothing but trouble. It all started when this king (who'd turned up uninvited with a right rowdy bunch) began complaining about being served with a slice of hot apple pie. He had the cheek to start giving orders. "A slice is no good to me," he boomed, "I want a full pie. And you can forget the apples. Bring me one with four and twenty blackbirds baked in it!"

Just then the cook came from the kitchen to tell me that one of the king's pals, a robber called the Knave of Hearts, had just made off with a full tray of tarts. Huh, the nerve of some people!

Next thing, there was a knock at the front door. Would you

believe it? An irate mother with three little girls, all blubbing their eyes out, and she's yelling at me.

"You and your wild parties! My little girls were just passing your front gate, when a fat little horror jumped out and kissed them. You can see how upset they are. I'm going to report this to the police!"

I tried to calm her down. "Madam, was this fat little boy eating a pudding and a pie by any chance?"

"That's him!" she shrieked. "He had a half-eaten treacle pudding, and a Christmas pie with a deep thumb mark in it!"

I took a look around and spotted him, lurking in some bushes next door. He thought I didn't recognise him, until I shouted, "Just you wait, Georgie! I'm going to tell your dad, Mr Porgey, all about your behaviour!"

I had to hurry back to the feast, then, because Simple Simon was on the phone, ringing up pie men all over town and ordering pies. Steak and kidney, cherry, rhubarb, and all kinds of other types. Lack of cash never bothered Simple Simon. He hadn't got a penny. So I had to grab the phone from him and cancel all the orders. Then I had to eject Old King Cole, for smoking his pipe at the table. But I let his Fiddlers Three stay – well, you need a bit of music at a feast, don't you? I like a bit of violin, though it's a shame they were drowned out by that weasel playing pop.

I was just thinking things couldn't get worse when Mary

Mary Quite Contrary came bustling in, roaring "You'd better come out into the back garden. I was just doing a table arrangement of silver bells and cockle shells, when guess that happened? Humpty Dumpty fell off your garden wall, and there's egg everywhere!"

I shook my head. "No way am I going out there. Humpty's been told time and again about climbing. It's his own fault."

But in the end I went out, of course, to see what I could do. Boy, was I sorry…

There was egg *everywhere*, plus a troop of king's horses and horsemen, galloping all over the place. The mess was unbelievable! Added to that, the three little pigs were squealing their heads off. They'd locked themselves in the garden shed, and the Big Bad Wolf was trying to blow it down. I was about to give him a swift kick in the tail, when he spotted a few lost sheep and charged off after them. I'm not saying a word if Little Bo Peep comes asking after them. I mean, what could one say? *Leave them alone and they'll come home, wagging their tails behind them?* Fat chance. There's no room for tail-wagging in a wolf's belly.

Well, that did it. I'd had enough of the Midnight Feast. I was trying to turf all my guests out, when the knock on the door came again. Two policemen this time. I tried explaining my situation. "Good evening officers, goodness, is that the time? Two a.m.? I hope the noise of my Midnight Feast didn't disturb the neighbours. Would you like to come in for coffee?"

The little vindictive-looking constable was scribbling furiously in his notebook. The big beefy unfriendly one did the talking. "I have to inform you, sir, of several reports. To whit, one Jack Horner alleges he was assaulted on your premises by a little old lady who gave her address as a shoe. Two, can you tell us the whereabouts of one Georgie Porgey, who is was involved in a mass kissing incident of various girls in the area, thirty six to date, all of which made their victims cry. We suspect he was driven to these acts by an overdose of puddings and pies, which he consumed on these premises. Then there are other charges to answer. The large dog you keep here, a.k.a. Big Bad Wolf. Caught with lots of sheep wool around his mouth, and Bo Peep's sheep are reported missing."

I interrupted at this point. "Yes, officer, but the three little pigs are safe." The little vindictive copper licked his pencil (like they usually do).

"Er, talking about pigs sir, is your name Mr Piper?"

I nodded and he smirked a satisfied smirk.

"We're holding your son down at the station for pig banditry. Can you confirm his name for us sir?"

I hung my head. "Yes, he's Tom. Tom the Piper's son."

So, dear Diary, it is now eleven a.m. and I am still down at the station, answering questions. I just overheard the desk Sergeant answering a phone call. It seems the Midnight Feast is still going full steam. The complaint was from a neighbour two doors away. A Wee Willie Winkie, in his nightgown, who can't get any sleep. My last Midnight Feast? Don't even ask!

THE LOST ART OF WORLD DOMINATION

Derek Landy

ith the shadows wrapped around him and the sliver of light falling dramatically over his eyes, the evil sorcerer Scaramouch Van Dreg stood in the dungeon and watched his captive with predatory amusement.

The dungeon was dark and damp and dank, and the chains that bound the skeleton detective were big and thick and heavy. They shackled the bones of his wrists to the stone floor, forcing him to kneel.

Scaramouch liked that. The great detective, the living skeleton who had foiled plan after plan, scheme after scheme, was now forced to look *up* at Scaramouch. Like he had always been meant to. Like *everyone* had always been meant to.

The detective, his dark blue suit burnt and torn and muddy, hadn't said anything for almost an hour. In fact, he hadn't *moved* for almost an hour. Scaramouch had been standing in the shadows, gloating, for a little over fifteen minutes, but he wasn't entirely sure that his captive had noticed.

He shifted his weight noisily, but the detective still did not acknowledge his presence.

Scaramouch frowned. There was very little point in going through all this if his efforts weren't rewarded with due and proper attention.

He brought himself up to his full height, which wasn't very high, and sucked in his belly, which was substantial. He gathered his cloak and stepped forward, gazing down at the top of the detective's skull with the pitiless gaze he had practised for hours.

"Skulduggery Pleasant," he sneered. "Finally, you are within my grasp."

The detective shifted slightly, and muttered something.

Good God. Was he *asleep*?

Scaramouch cleared his throat and gave the detective a little kick. The detective jerked awake and looked around for a moment, then looked up with those empty eye sockets.

"Oh," he said, like he had just met a casual acquaintance on the street, "hello."

Unsure how to counter this unexpected approach to being a captive, Scaramouch decided to replay the sneer.

"Skulduggery Pleasant," he repeated. "Finally, you are within my grasp."

"It does appear so," Pleasant agreed, nodding. "And in a dungeon, no less. How brilliantly postmodern of you."

"You have interfered in my plans for the last time," Scaramouch continued. "Unfortunately for you, you will not live to regret your mistake."

Pleasant tilted his head curiously. "Scaramouch? Scaramouch Van Dreg? Is that you?"

Scaramouch smiled nastily. "Oh yes. You have fallen into the clutches of your deadliest enemy."

"What are *you* doing here?"

Scaramouch's smile faltered. "What?"

"How are you mixed up in all this?"

"How am I...? What do you mean? This is *my* plot."

"*You're* plotting to use the Crystal of the Saints to bring the Faceless Ones back into our reality?"

Scaramouch frowned. "What? No. What do the Faceless Ones have to do with this? I don't want the Faceless Ones back, I don't even worship them. No, this plot is for *me*, to gain absolute power."

"Then... you're not in league with Rancid Fines or Christophe Nocturnal?"

"I've never even *met* Rancid Fines," Scaramouch said, "and I *hate* Christophe Nocturnal."

Pleasant absorbed this information with a nod. "In that case, I'm afraid there's been a bit of a misunderstanding."

Scaramouch felt like he'd been punched in the gut. All the breath left him, and his shoulders slumped. "You mean, you're not here for me?"

"Dreadfully sorry," Pleasant said.

"But... but you arrived at the hotel. You and your partner, the girl. You were asking all those questions."

"We were looking for Fines and Nocturnal. We didn't even know you were in the country. To be honest with you, and I don't mean to offend you or anything, but I thought you had passed away some time ago."

Scaramouch gaped. "I just took a little break..."

Pleasant shrugged. "Well, at least now I know. So what are you up to these days?"

"I'm... I have plans," Scaramouch said, dejected.

"The absolute power thing you mentioned?"

Scaramouch nodded.

"And how's that going?"

"It's going OK, I suppose. I mean, you know, everything's

on schedule and proceeding apace…"

"Well that's good. We all need something to get us up in the mornings, am I right? We all need goals."

"Yeah." An unwelcome thought seeped into Scaramouch's mind and lingered there. He tried ignoring it but it flickered and swam, and finally he had to ask; "You don't view me as your deadliest enemy, do you?"

Pleasant hesitated. His skull remained as impassive as ever, but this hesitation spoke volumes. "I view you as *a* deadly enemy," he said helpfully.

"How deadly?"

"I don't know… relatively?"

"Relatively deadly? That's all? I thought we were arch-enemies."

"Oh," Pleasant said. "No, I wouldn't call us *arch*-enemies. Nefarian Serpine was an arch-enemy. Mevolent, obviously. A few others."

"But not us?"

"Not really…"

"Why? Is it because I'm not powerful enough?"

"No, not exactly."

"Then why? What's so different between me and, say, Serpine?"

"Well," said Pleasant, "Serpine had options. He was adaptable.

Remember, the deadliest enemies are not necessarily the strongest, they're the smartest."

"So it's because I'm not *smart* enough? But I *am* smart! I am highly intelligent!"

"OK," Pleasant said in an understanding voice.

"Don't patronise me!" Scaramouch snapped. "I have *you* as a prisoner, don't I? You fell into my trap without even a hint of a suspicion!"

"It *was* a clever trap."

"And those chains that bind your powers — you think that's easy to do? You think *that* doesn't require intelligence?"

"No no," Pleasant said, "I have to admit, you got me fair and square."

"You're damn right I did," Scaramouch sneered. "And you don't even know about my plot yet, do you? You don't even know how intelligent *that* is."

"Well, like I said, I've been busy—"

"Busy with Fines, and with Nocturnal, busy with the threat of the Faceless Ones — but you haven't been busy with the *real* threat, have you?"

"I suppose not," Pleasant said, and then added, "You mean you, don't you?"

"Of course I mean me! I've been smart enough to fool you all into thinking I was dead. I've been smart enough to work under your radar, to set in motion events that will grant me absolute power, which will lead to my total dominion over this world! Now *that*, detective, *that* is smart!"

"Total dominion?"

"Oh yes, skeleton. How does it feel to know that an opponent such as I, an adversary you would have classified as merely 'relatively deadly', will soon rule this planet with a will of iron, and a fist of…" He faltered. "…iron."

"Um…"

"What?"

"I was just going to say, have you really thought this through?"

"What do you mean?"

"You're talking about ruling the world, right?"

"Yes."

"Not bringing back old gods, not turning the world into some new version of hell, not remaking it as you see fit…"

"Well, no."

"You're just talking about ruling it, then?"

"Yes. With a will of iron and a fist of iron."

"Yes. And again, I'm compelled to ask — have you really thought this through?"

Scaramouch pinched the bridge of his nose with his thumb and forefinger. He was getting a headache. He could feel it coming on. "What do you mean? What is so wrong with planning to rule the world?"

"Well, for a start, think of all the work."

"I'll have minions," Scaramouch said dismissively.

"But they'll still need orders. They'll need you to tell them what to do. You'll be inundated with reports, with documents, with briefings. There won't be enough hours in the day to go over them all, let alone make any decisions."

"Then I'll just order that the days be longer," Scaramouch said. "I will decree that a day stops and starts when *I* decide, not the sun or the moon."

"And how will you cope with warring nations?"

Scaramouch laughed. "When I am ruler, there will be no wars. Everyone will do what I tell them."

"There are billions of people in the world, all with their own viewpoints, all with their own rights. It won't be as simple as telling them to just *stop*. What about famine?"

"What about it?"

"What will you do about it?"

"I'm not sure I understand."

"If famine strikes a country, what will you do?"

Scaramouch smiled evilly. "Maybe I will do nothing. Maybe I will let the country die."

"In which case, you will have an entire country rise against you, because they have nothing left to lose."

"Then I will destroy them."

"And you'll have to deal with the neighbouring countries squabbling over the remains."

"Then I'll destroy them – no, I'll order them to… they'll do what I tell them, alright?"

"And the media?"

Scaramouch sighed. "What about them?"

"How will you cope with the media questioning your policies?"

"There will be no questions. This won't be a democracy, it will be a dictatorship."

"There will be always be dissent."

"What did I say? I'll have minions, I told you. *They'll* take care of any rebels."

"You'll have a secret police?"

"Of course!"

"You'll assign minions to levels of power?"

"Naturally!"

"And when these minions get ambitions of their own, and they go to overthrow you?"

"Then I'll kill them!" Scaramouch said, exasperated. "I'll have absolute power, remember?"

"And how do you plan to attain this absolute power?"

"It's all in my plan!" Scaramouch yelled, pacing to the wall of the dungeon.

"What about sorcerers?"

Scaramouch tore the cloak from around his neck. It was heavy, and too warm, and when he paced it was annoying. "What about the bloody sorcerers?"

Pleasant's chains jangled slightly as he shrugged. "You don't really think they'll just stand back and let this happen, do you? I realise I'll be dead, so that's one less you'll have to worry about, but there are plenty more."

"There won't be," Scaramouch said, stepping back into the shadows for dramatic affect. "When my plan is complete, I will be the only one capable of wielding magic."

"So you're going to kill them all?"

"I won't have to. They will be left as ordinary mortals, while I will be filled with their powers."

"Ah," Pleasant said. "OK."

"Now do you appreciate my vast and superior intelligence?"

Pleasant thought for a moment. "Yes," he decided.

"Excellent. I'm sorry we can't talk further, detective, but my Hour of Glory is at hand, and your death will be—"

"One more question."

Scaramouch's chin dropped to his chest. "What?" he asked bleakly.

"On the surface, this plot is fine. Drain the magic from others, and then use this magic to become all-powerful and unstoppable and take over the world. I can't see anything wrong with that plot – in theory. But my question, Scaramouch, is how exactly are you going to achieve all this?"

Scaramouch picked his cloak off the ground, felt through it until he came to the cleverly concealed pocket. From this pocket he withdrew a small wooden box with a metal clasp.

He held the box for Pleasant to see. "Recognise this?"

Pleasant peered closer, examining the etchings in the wood. "Ohhh," he said, impressed.

"Exactly. This container, enchanted with twenty-three spells from twenty-three mages, is one of the fabled Lost Artifacts. I have spent the last fifteen months tracking it down – and tonight, it is finally mine."

"So it's true, then?"

"Of course it's true. Why wouldn't it be?"

Pleasant's head jerked up sharply. "You mean you haven't checked it?"

Scaramouch suddenly felt a little foolish. "I—I don't have to," he said. "Everyone knows—"

"Oh Scaramouch," Pleasant said, disappointment in his voice.

"I just got it!" Scaramouch said defensively. "Literally, I just got it three hours ago!"

"And you haven't checked it?"

"I didn't have *time*. I had to capture *you*."

Pleasant looked back at the box, and his head tilted thoughtfully. "If that *is* the box from the Lost Artifacts, and it certainly does *look* like it might be authentic, then it contains an insect with the power to drain magic at a bite."

"Exactly."

"Providing that insect is still inside."

Scaramouch looked at the box. "There are no holes in it."

"It's been lost for three hundred years."

"But the insect's meant to live forever, right? It doesn't need food or anything?"

"Well, that's the legend. Can you hear it? You should be able to hear it buzzing around in there."

Scaramouch shook the box, and held it up to his ear. "Nothing," he said.

"Well, it's a thick box," Pleasant said. "You probably wouldn't be able to hear it anyway."

Scaramouch shook it again, then listened for any buzzing. Even a single buzz. Anything.

"Did you pay much for it?" Pleasant asked.

"The guy who found it, he needed to mount expeditions and things. It wasn't cheap."

"How much did he charge?"

"I, uh, I gave him everything I had."

The detective went quiet.

"But I'm going to be ruler of the world!" Scaramouch explained. "What difference does it make to me?"

"He made an awful lot of money by just handing over a box, without even verifying that it contained what you hope it contains."

"How will I know?"

"There's only one way. You have to open it."

"But the insect will fly away!"

"Let it out near me," the skeleton suggested. "You're going to kill me anyway, right? So what do I care if it drains my powers before I die?"

Scaramouch narrowed his eyes. "Why would you make this offer?"

"Because I'm *curious*. Scaramouch, I'm a detective. I solve mysteries. If my final act in this world is to establish whether or not a mythological insect could still be contained in one of the Lost Artifacts, then that, to me, would be a good death."

Scaramouch looked at him, and nodded. "OK."

"Put it on the ground, open it, and stand back. When it's finished draining me, it'll be sluggish. That's when you recapture it."

Scaramouch nodded. He licked his lips nervously, and placed the box on the floor. He undid the metal clasp, felt his heart pound in his chest, and opened the lid.

He scampered back into the shadows.

The detective gazed down into the box.

"Well?" Scaramouch asked from the corner.

"Can't see anything," Pleasant said. "It's a little dark... wait."

"Yes? What?"

And then, the most beautiful sound Scaramouch had ever heard – a buzzing.

"Amazing," Pleasant said in a whisper.

Something rose from the box, rising into the air after centuries of being trapped. It was unsteady, and weak, but it flew. It *lived*.

"One little insect," Pleasant was saying. "The legends say it rose from the carcass of a slain demon. An insect borne of evil, and wickedness, the demon's last attempt to destroy its enemies." The insect flew up, dancing in a shaft of light. "One little insect, and it could be responsible for bringing this world to its knees."

"Wonderful," Scaramouch breathed.

The insect landed on the ground in front of its box, its prison for all those years. Pleasant looked down at it, then moved slightly and knelt on the insect and squished it.

Scaramouch screamed and the door burst open and Valkyrie Cain stepped into the dungeon.

"What the hell is going on here?" she asked.

Scaramouch charged at her and the girl closed her eyes and flexed her fingers. Her eyes and hand snapped open and the air around her rippled. Scaramouch was hurled back off his feet. He crashed into the far wall, hitting his head and collapsing with a groan. He heard the girl and the detective talking, and he heard the chains being unlocked. Moaning, he turned over and looked up at them.

"It was a trick," he said. "You really *were* here to stop me, weren't you? You really *were* here to foil my plan. This is the last time, you hear me? I will escape whatever prison you send me to, and the next time we meet you will pay for—"

"Who's this?" Valkyrie Cain asked.

Scaramouch paled. "What? What do you mean who am I?"

"His name's Scaramouch Van Dreg," Pleasant told her.

"She knows who I am!" Scaramouch shrieked. "I am your deadliest enemy!"

Cain raised an eyebrow but ignored him. "Has he got anything to do with Fines and Nocturnal?"

"Nope."

"Then why are we wasting our time? Come on, we've got real bad guys to stop."

Cain walked out. Skulduggery Pleasant looked down at Scaramouch and shrugged.

"I'll just chain you up for the moment, but the Cleavers will be around soon to take you into custody. Is that alright with you?"

Scaramouch started crying.

"Good man. Don't let this get you down though. We all need goals, and I fully expect to do battle with you again, OK?"

Scaramouch wailed.

"We need more villains like you, you know that? We need more bad guys who want to take over the world. There aren't enough of them. The others think it's just, you know... *silly*."

Scaramouch felt the shackles on his wrists. He had to look up to watch Skulduggery Pleasant leave the dungeon.

DANSE MACABRE

Katherine Langrish

"Can't we go now?" Philip whined.

"Hush!" said Mum.

He hadn't been that loud. It was just that in this dim, cold abbey, every sound was magnified. Even a whisper rustled around the walls. A cough made you jump nearly out of your skin. Every shuffling footstep woke echoes that scurried off across the floor to bury themselves in nooks and crannies and little dark spaces. Philip ached to go outside, where the little lizards flickered over the hot stone steps in the sunshine.

His parents had stopped at another tomb, a sort of stone box with a statue of some old bishop lying flat on top of it, scowling at the roof. His face looked like a cake of dirty soap, half rubbed away by time. Philip shivered.

"Dad," he pleaded again. "Can't we go?"

Dr Acton frowned. "Try and take an interest, Phil."

"He's only eight." Mum said apologetically.

Dad taught history in a university. He always wanted Philip to like old things. Now he gave an impatient sigh. "Well – we can't go without seeing the Danse Macabre. It's the reason I came. Besides, it's something exciting for a boy. Skeletons, Phil! You'll like that, won't you?"

"Real skeletons?" Philip hung back. Mum laughed. "Of course not, silly." (Though why was it silly? There must be hundreds of skeletons in a place like this.) "It's a painting." Mum went on, "a wonderful painting. Come and see."

She led him into a dismally lit side aisle and clasped her hands. "Here it is!"

There were marks on the plaster, but Philip couldn't see them properly till his father came back with one of the guides – a tall monk in a grey robe. The monk had a torch. He switched it on and danced it over the wall. Out sprang a horrible face – bald, bony, with hollow eyes and grinning teeth.

For a second Philip nearly shrieked – but it was just a painting. The light travelled down over a laddery chest, pinched waist and long spidery legs, then swung up to show that the creature had its arms round some person wearing a cloak and a crown. It appeared to be doing a dance step.

"Un cadavre et l'Empereur," said the monk. He glanced at Philip and dropped into English. "The Dance of Death, m'sieur, m'dame. Many such paintings were made after the Great Plague. Here you see Death meeting a king, bishop, knight, peasant – all the estates."

He swung the torch along the dirty plaster wall to pick out a procession of figures: people being waylaid by skeletons. The skeletons weren't nice clean Hallowe'en bones. Their spindly limbs were clothed in withered flesh. They seemed vigorous with awful glee as they linked arms with the living to yank them away into the dance of shadows. And the living figures stood in frozen sadness at the surprise of death.

"Wonderful!" Dad paced along the wall, studying each of the groups. "Look at this one, Becky!" He stopped near the end of the fresco, where one of the Deaths was bending down coaxingly to a little child, hiding its pitiless face behind one crooked elbow, stretching out its other arm to touch...

"Oh!" Mum sounded breathless and odd. She glanced quickly at Philip, stepping forward to block his view. "Perhaps it's not really suitable, after all..."

Dad wasn't listening. "The painting is unfinished?" he asked the monk.

"Oui, monsieur. The drawings were made in charcoal, the background was painted in. But the artist went no further. The clothes, the faces, the figures were left as you see them — sketches, without colour."

"Why?"

The monk shrugged. "It is a mystery. No one knows."

"Are there no records? When was this painted?"

"In the time of Abbot Renaud, it is thought. Perhaps about 1480. But nothing is known of the artist. He may have been a monk here…"

He droned on. Bored beyond words, Philip saw something like a stone bed sticking out from the wall. There was even a stone pillow at one end, and a strange hole, like the plug hole in a bath, at the other. Intrigued, he sat on the stone edge and poked a pencil down the hole to see how deep it was. He felt the point go into something soft. Chewing gum? No: this felt mushy.

"Get up! You mustn't sit there!" the monk shouted.

Philip leaped up and dropped the pencil. It rolled into a gloomy corner and he scrambled after it. He hated the abbey, he hated the monk. In revenge he picked up the pencil and scrawled his name on the wall:

Philip Acton

His scream shocked the echoing spaces of the abbey. All the murmuring and whispering and fidgeting went small and still. Then his parents came running to shake, snatch and scold him.

"How could you, Philip? To scribble on a wall – in a church, of all places – defacing a wonderful fresco—" Dr Acton drew a disbelieving breath. "What were you thinking?"

Philip shook his head

"I'll take him out," said Mum quietly.

In the strong, comforting sunshine, they waited for Dad to finish apologising to the monks. Philip hung his head while Mum ranted. "I don't care how bored you were; there's no excuse. And, goodness, what's this on your trousers? It's all black and sticky." She whipped out a tissue and rubbed. "It won't come off. It's some kind of tar, I believe – and it smells revolting. You've got it on your fingers too. Where did it come from?"

"I don't know. My pencil," he said, pulling it out of his pocket.

"Throw it away!" She twitched it from his hand and sent it spinning down the steps, adding more gently, "But what made you scream?"

"A nasty man," he whispered.

Unexpectedly, Mum was silent. "Those paintings," she said at last. "I'm sorry, Phil. They were nasty, I agree."

"Mum—"

"Don't think any more about them." She gave him a brief hug. "We'll do something nice this afternoon." She turned as Dad emerged from the cold mouth of the abbey door. "Were they very angry, Paul?"

"It's worked out well!" Dad was looking gleeful. "Phil's silly pencil marks will wipe off easily enough. And I've made an appointment for later today. That monk who showed us round turns out to be the abbey librarian. So I just happened to mention that I was *Dr* Acton, a historian – and he's offered to let me look through the old manuscripts in the library! How about that?"

"Lovely," Mum sighed.

That afternoon she and Philip went riding on rough little ponies through the resinous sunlit glades of the pinewoods. It was a treat he knew he ought to enjoy. But the sunshine dazzled his eyes, and his head ached. By suppertime he felt worse. Their guesthouse was in the village, only a few crooked streets from the abbey. Madame Bertrand, the proprietress, was concerned for Philip.

"He is pale, it is no good for children to look so. Can you not eat the tart, mon lapin? Non? Ah, quel dommage!"

Philip ducked his head and wished she would leave him alone.

"Bedtime," said Mum rather grimly. She took Philip up to the room they shared. There was a big four-poster bed for his parents, and a small couch against the wall for Philip. The ceiling sagged, the walls bulged as if the whole room might implode with age. Up till now Philip had liked it. He hadn't minded being left there while Mum and Dad had a last drink and an evening stroll. Tonight—

"Don't go," he begged, grabbing Mum's hand.

"Now what's wrong?" she asked, ruffling his hair. "You're not frightened, are you? Are you?" He nodded. "But what of?"

"That man I saw in the abbey," he muttered sullenly, picking at the covers.

"Oh Philip, it was only a picture, not a very nice one, but just a picture."

"It wasn't a picture. He spoke to me."

"What?... In English?"

Philip looked confused. "No – I don't know. But he did speak. He said, 'I shall come and get you.' And I didn't like it. He hadn't got any lips."

Mum drew a sharp breath. "Oh Phil. What an imagination you have! You saw a nasty old wall painting, that's all... Now lie down and go to sleep."

When Philip's mother finally got back to her congealing dinner, she sat down crossly.

"Those paintings in the abbey have scared Philip silly. He thinks he saw a nasty man who said, 'I shall come and get you.' I suppose he overheard the monk arranging to meet you this afternoon."

"Impossible," said Dr Acton. "Philip wasn't there. We made the arrangements later, remember? You'd taken him out."

Mrs Acton banged her coffee cup down. "He's only eight. You can't expect him to enjoy trailing round old abbeys. If you'd pay a bit more attention to him, Paul..."

They went up to bed early, annoyed with each other. Philip was asleep. Dr Acton soon began snoring, but his wife lay half dozing, repeating to herself some of the choice things she had said. Pretty soon she drifted into a sort of dream. She was lying back to back with her husband, but in the dream it was not him. It was someone else – someone long and stringy, who would presently turn and wind leathery arms around her...

She struggled out of sleep with a muffled shriek and sat up in the darkness. Philip was tossing and moaning. She was about to get up and go to him – when she heard scratching at the outside of their bedroom door.

The cat?

She didn't believe it was a cat. The door was old and loose-fitting. A clumsy bolt prevented it from drifting open in the middle of the night. The door rattled softly and the old-fashioned latch clicked as it lifted and dropped, but the bolt held. Then there was more rattling and scratching, as though something were picking at the edges of the door. It went on for some time, then gave up. After a moment, as if trying one last thing, there came a quiet, stealthy knock.

She sat, frozen. But the knock was not repeated. It was much, much later before she could get to sleep.

Next morning at breakfast, pleasant Madame Bertrand was in a bad mood. Setting the croissants abruptly on the table, she launched into forthright French.

She was sorry to say it, but le petit Philip must have brought something in on his shoes yesterday. This morning she had found the passage covered with dirty marks, leading up the stone staircase to just outside their door. She had had to scrub the steps on her knees, and it was hard to remove, black and sticky, and of an 'odeur pestilentiel'. She could not allow such a thing to occur again.

"I'm very sorry, Madame," said Dr Acton. "Philip, what do you know about this?" But Philip knew nothing. He looked pale, with black rings under his eyes. He said he had had bad dreams: *that man* had been trying to get into the room during the night.

"Perhaps it's his footprints," he said with a hysterical laugh. His parents looked at him uneasily, and Madame Bertrand suddenly patted him on the shoulder.

"La, la, la," she said. "It matters nothing. You are tired, mon pauvre. Boys should not be tired. Now, m'sieur" – she turned to Dr Acton – "do not take him to the abbey. Let him run about in the sunshine. It will be better." She beckoned Philip. "Viens, mon petit. Come with me, I have a sucette for you," and she led him away to the kitchen to give him sweets.

"Well," Dr Acton cleared his throat, "I must be off to the abbey. Yesterday I saw some fascinating old rolls of accounts, which can't have been touched for years. And I didn't tell you last night, but we found an item relating to the fresco. Someone called Jehan le Necre – 'Black John' – was given money 'at the command of Abbot Renaud, to pay for a great brush of hogshair and two others of squirrel, for the Danse Macabre on the wall west of the choir.' Of course we don't know if he was the painter. But it's likely, it's likely."

"That's wonderful," said Mrs Acton absently. "Paul, why did the monk yesterday make Philip get off that little stone bed?"

"Ah – that." Dr Acton looked uncomfortable. "It's not a bed, you see, though of course a child would think it was. It's a medieval funerary bench – a mortuary slab. They laid out all the dead monks there. That's a drainage hole at the bottom end."

His wife shuddered. "Paul, Madame Bertrand is right. From now on, Philip and I are staying out of the abbey."

She took Philip on a picnic. They climbed the hill above the village. While Mum sat watching the cloud shadows chase over the sloping fields, Philip played football with some English boys whose parents had stopped their car nearby.

"We're staying at a campsite," the boys boasted. "It's great, there's a swimming pool and table tennis, and barbecues every night. Is it just you and your mum? Where are you staying?"

"Down there," Philip pointed. "In the village of La Chaise Dieu. My dad's working in the big abbey. Can you see the roof?"

"In the abbey? Weird! Is he religious or something?"

"No," said Philip. "He just likes history."

When the boys left, he said wistfully, "I wish we could go camping."

Mum sighed. "I don't know, Phil. Maybe next year. If Dad agrees."

The wind had whipped colour into Philip's face and his eyes were brighter. But when she tucked him into bed that evening, he held her hand more tightly than ever and looked at her pleadingly.

"Phil—" She didn't know what to do. "We're only downstairs. We'll be coming to bed later, you won't be alone. How I wish we'd never taken you into the abbey. Are you *still* scared of that painting?"

He shook his head. "I'm afraid of that man." His lips trembled and his eyelashes were suddenly spiky and wet. He put his arms around her and buried his face.

"Philip, dear…" She hugged him back. "You're quite safe. Shall I stay till you go to sleep?"

He shook his head again. Just as she got to the door he said in a flat, tired voice, "It wouldn't help. He won't come till after you've gone."

She went back, held his hand, looked him in the eye. "Philip. *Listen* to me. *Nobody* is going to come. Nothing bad is going to happen. I promise. I promise! Now lie down and go to sleep."

He was tired after all, and it didn't take long. When she saw him breathing peacefully, she drew the covers up and switched off the light.

Downstairs, Dr Acton was excited. "We've found out more. The Abbot himself is interested now. It really was 'Black John' who made the Danse. But we don't know much about him. He was probably a monk from another monastery, on loan, as it were, to do the work. He was a brilliant artist, but a bit of a troublemaker. Malicious. The other monks complained to the abbot that he quarrelled in the cloisters and 'disturbs our peace'. Perhaps they got tired of him, you see, and sent him away. That could be why the fresco was never finished!"

"I wish it had never been begun," said his wife whole-heartedly. "It has scared Philip stiff. And I slept badly last night myself."

"It's strong stuff," Dr Acton admitted. "Intended to be. I'm not surprised he's nervous; it even affected me. While the Abbot and I were deciphering the Latin, he left the room to fetch something. I was sure I was not alone. I kept twisting about to see who was watching me, and I could swear I heard a voice whisper in a very strange accent, 'Je vous mène à la Danse'. The Abbot came back in then, but it wasn't him."

"What does that mean?" asked Mrs Acton apprehensively.

"Oh, 'I will lead you in the dance,' or, 'take you to the dance,' I suppose. It was simply my mind playing tricks; there was no one there."

"Paul—" Mrs Acton swallowed, and stopped.

"No, no, no!" cried Dr Acton, smacking his hand on the table. "And to show you all's well, we'll go for an evening walk. Yes, now! You mustn't let yourself get into a silly, superstitious panic. We'll walk down towards the abbey and back. It's a lovely evening."

They set off arm in arm down the narrow street. Few people were about. The uneven roofs showed dark against a clear sky in which tremulous stars were opening. In the square, they looked up at the mighty bulk of the Abbey, reared high on its great flights of steps. The tall windows glimmered. Suddenly they heard a wonderful sound – a sonorous humming that rose and sank, musical as a hive. The monks, chanting their evening prayers.

"Oh, you're right, Paul," Mrs Acton said softly. "No harm could come out of a place like this."

They walked slowly past, listening. "We must go back. Philip might wake," she said at last. As they turned to go back, something slipped from the dark Abbey doorway and scuttled down the steps. It was too dark to be sure...

"A very big dog?" said Dr Acton.

"It moved like a spider," said his wife with a shiver. They could not see where it had gone. "Let's hurry," she said, grasping his hand.

The street was quiet. Ahead of them, someone else was out late. They could see his shoulders and head in silhouette, bobbing along about fifty metres ahead of them. He seemed very tall and thin, and, as he passed below a street lamp, *wasp-waisted*. "Isn't there something odd about that chap—" began Dr Acton, but his wife did not reply. She tore her hand free from his and began to run.

With some dread knowledge stirring within him, he started after her. She was sprinting up the road, hair flying; nevertheless he gained on her with his long strides. Beyond, the figure she was pursuing passed below another lamp, and the head gleamed bald. It turned at the door of the guesthouse and vanished inside.

Acton crashed past his wife in the doorway and leaped up the stairs three at a time. The treads were patched and soiled, and the door handle was sticky. He burst into the bedroom, hearing his wife sobbing as she clawed her way up behind him.

Philip lay asleep. Poised above him was the corrupt creature, spindly and bedraggled as some oiled bird dragged from a slick. Jerkily it reached out, hesitated. Delicately it hid its face in the crook of one arm. The other hand plucked at Philip.

There were two screams: Philip, waking, and his mother rushing in. She pushed the creature violently aside and threw herself at Philip, trying to shield him and hold him at the same time. Philip's eyes were like black pennies in his white face. "You said he wouldn't come!" he shrieked, half sobbing. "Mummy, you *promised!*"

Acton turned upon the thing, which had fallen and was crawling brokenly in the corner. "Go!" he stammered in unspeakable horror. "Go away!"

Footsteps thudded on the stairs. A tall man strode into the room in a swirl of grey robes, one commanding hand lifting a crucifix. Behind him Madame Bertrand came puffing, shocked and open-mouthed. "By the power invested in me as Abbot," said the man firmly, in Latin, "and in the name of the Father, Son and Holy Spirit, begone from this place to the place prepared for you. Go, and never return."

Madame Bertrand was wonderful. After a single glance at the

mess on the floor, she swept them all into her private sitting room, where she plied them with tiny glasses of old cognac, strong and aromatic enough to exorcise any number of ghosts. And Philip and his mother, who were nearly fainting, revived enough to hear how the Abbot, who had been reading the old rolls, had discovered something so interesting that he wanted to show it to Dr Acton straight away, late as it was. It was a piece of loose parchment, 'possibly in Abbot Renaud's own hand,' and translated it ran:

"By my command the Danse Macabre is to be left uncompleted. For since the death of the painter, no one will undertake to begin where he left off, saying that he is as jealous in death as he was in life, and will not suffer another hand so much as to touch his work. They say the Evil One came to claim him. And this is more credible because while he was with us, he never ceased cursing and blaspheming. Therefore the Danse shall remain unfinished, to remind all beholders of the arresting hand of Death, who comes in the midst of life." And in smaller handwriting is an annotation:

"He died of the plague, but does not rest."

Philip recovered slowly. His parents took him away and watched over him anxiously. They promised to take him to a campsite next year — "No more abbeys."

Their nerves were badly shaken, and they both had bad dreams. "But it will fade," Dr Acton said to his wife. "It must fade — in time, you know. And after all, my dear — thank heavens — we never saw its face."

Margaret Mahy

THE UNEXPECTED FAIRY GODMOTHER

Peter was a very lucky boy. He had a fairy godmother. She lived beside the railway station, and when he was going into town and had to catch a train he often visited her at the same time. She would give him orange juice and cake and they talked of many things. The only trouble with his fairy godmother was that she was very, very, very well-behaved, and she wanted Peter to be very well-behaved too. She wanted him to be neat and tidy, not just every now and then, but all the time. She wanted him to enjoy school and ask the teacher for more homework every night. Sometimes she would grant him a wish, but it was only ever a very small one.

One day Peter visited her and she gave him a wish in a small egg-shaped box.

"Be careful with it, won't you?" she said with a saintly smile. "Times are hard for fairy godmothers these days. I don't have as many wishes to give away as I used to."

She was wearing her usual fairy godmother clothes: a long pink frilly dress, wings made out of silver paper and ballet shoes. However you couldn't help noticing that she had a black eye patch and a mermaid tattooed on her arm. She was always trying to pull her sleeve down over this tattoo. She didn't like anyone to see it.

"Thank you," Peter said, putting the wish in his pocket. "I have to go and catch the train now. See you soon."

"Trains!" said his godmother. "I like ships better."

She pulled the sleeve down over the tattoo again.

"But you can't go to town in a ship," Peter said.

"I know," she said sadly. "I used to go everywhere by pumpkin, but now I'm stuck in the present day nothing works the way it used to. Trains give me a headache. Things are not easy for fairy godmothers, I can tell you that."

Peter felt rather sorry for her. He left her sticking silver paper from a packet of chocolate over a hole in one of her wings. He forgot the wish, which was still in his pocket.

Perhaps there is something about carrying a wish in your

pocket that helps you to see unexpected things. When Peter got to the railway station he found a very strange train waiting there – an old-fashioned train with a long slim funnel and a silver bell. It was green, but it didn't look as if it had been painted green. It looked as if it was covered in moss. Still, it was a train, no doubt about that, and it was waiting at the platform and pointing in the right direction.

All around it stood an angry crowd of people waving flags and banners, and the longer Peter looked at them, the stranger he realised they were, even though he could only see bits of them because of the flags and banners. They seemed to be a crowd of old men and women wearing dressing-gowns or maybe robes, covered with pictures of moons and stars, as well as numbers and triangles and circles. Peter read the signs on a nearby banner: *Cutting a wizard's railway service makes a wizard cross and nervous.*

Peter did not like the idea of a cross, nervous wizard. He saw that the woman holding this banner seemed to have grass instead of hair. There were even daisies in it. The stationmaster was standing there trying to explain something to them.

"Ladies and gentlemen…" he began, but there was a growl of resentment. "That is to say wizards and magicians…" he hastily corrected himself. "I am sorry to say that this will be the last Wizard's Train running back into past time. The service is too expensive."

"But we need our train," shouted a wizard with a nose like two potatoes stuck end to end. "How will we get back into the past without our train?"

"You can get back into the past all right," said the stationmaster. "This last train will stop at all centuries back to the fourth century AD. After that you will have to walk. However, you will not be able to come back to the present day. You will have to get work in the past."

"But my specialty is computer games. I'm a computer wizard," cried one wizard, who was very respectably dressed. "There is no work for a computer wizard in the past."

"Then stay here," said the stationmaster. "Though there will be no train tomorrow. The service is definitely being cancelled."

"But my wife and children live in the eighteenth century," cried the computer wizard. Several other wizards growled like dogs. Things began to look nasty. Peter had never seen such a thing at the railway station before.

"The service is not paying!" cried the stationmaster. "There are not enough of you. Besides," he added crossly, "some of you pay with fairy gold, and that turns into leaves the following day. No wonder we are running at a terrible loss."

At this moment a wonderful idea occurred to Peter.

"Excuse me," he cried. Everyone turned to look at him. "Do you let fairy godmothers on your train?"

There was a howl of fury.

"Fairy godmothers!" shouted a wizard who seemed to be covered in green scales. "Let that lot of goody-goodies on our train? Never!"

"Well, they are stuck in the present day," Peter shouted back. "And they can't travel by pumpkin any more. They wouldn't be any trouble."

But there were cries of "No! No! They'll want us to be neat and tidy. They will always be trying to make us behave well. We don't want that."

Some of the wizards began to look at Peter in a dangerous way, as if they were planning to cast a spell on him. Everyone was shouting. The stationmaster sighed, and mopped his forehead with his handkerchief, but there must have been magic about because his face turned bright blue. Peter thought anything could happen at any moment.

I wish there was a way out of this, he thought, putting his hands in his pockets. Immediately he felt the small egg-shaped box his fairy godmother had given him. He took it out and opened it, but there was nothing in it but a rather nice picture of his fairy godmother... his fairy godmother dressed as a *pirate*. A wizard, who had grabbed his shoulder from behind, looked at the picture and gave a cry of surprise.

"How do you come to have a photograph of Mad Meg

Moggins, the Coromandel pirate?" he cried.

"This isn't Mad Meg Moggins," said Peter. "It's my fairy godmother." But then he suddenly remembered the black eye patch and her tattooed mermaid.

"It *is* Mad Meg Moggins," cried another wizard, snatching the photograph. It was passed around amongst the wizards, and one and all agreed that it was Mad Meg Moggins, no doubt about it.

"Fancy Mad Meg Moggins turning out to be a fairy godmother," cried one wizard who had rollerskates instead of feet.

"Being a fairy godmother is probably just part-time work," said another.

"Yes," said a third, "this proves that fairy godmothers are just as bad as the rest of us."

"If they're just as bad as the rest of us," cried a fourth wizard, "we can let them on our train."

"And the more people that travel on the train, the more the service will pay," cried the stationmaster. "We may be able to keep the train going after all."

At that moment the silver bell rang and there was a great rush of wizards to get on to the train, so Peter never quite heard what was decided. His own train came into the station and he got on it and went two stations down the line to football practice.

The next time Peter went to visit his godmother, he saw she

was looking much more cheerful. Her pink dress and ballet shoes were all sparkly. She was walking around on tiptoe and waving her wand. Her wings looked in much better condition. Of course, she still had her eye patch, and under her sleeve he could see the tail of the tattooed mermaid.

"Are you travelling by pumpkin again?" he asked her.

"No – I've bought a season ticket on a very nice train," she said. "It's much more comfortable than the usual kind."

Peter thought a bit. "Godmother," he said. "Have you ever heard of anyone called Mad Meg Moggins, the Coromandel pirate?" His fairy godmother started violently. Then she blushed all over. Even her pink sparkly dress turned quite red.

"Never mention a pirate to a fairy godmother," she cried. "It brings on my hay fever. Here! Take this wish – good for an ice-cream at any store down the street – and leave me alone to do my politeness exercises."

As Peter took the wish, he noticed she was wearing a pink, sparkly sword at her side... not at all the sort of thing you would expect from your average fairy godmother.

David Mackintosh

Garth Nix

THE DAY I CAUGHT A GIANT OCTOPUS

I've been fishing with my father since I was about six or seven, so right now that means we've been fishing together for more than thirty-five years. He nearly always catches more fish than I do, or else he just catches bigger ones, usually at the last moment when I finally think that I might come out ahead.

But my dad has never caught an octopus bigger than he is, and I have. Well, it was bigger than a nine-year-old boy, and "caught" is perhaps not quite accurate, as you will hear.

We were fishing from an old ruined jetty that had once thrust out a lot further into the bay. It had been used for loading timber from a sawmill on the point that had burned down in the 1920s.

There wasn't anything left of the sawmill, and not much of the jetty. It was just a few planks rotting between the surviving concrete piers, so you had to be careful where you walked or stood.

There'd been a few bream caught that morning, bright silver shapes easily seen in the clear, blue-green water below the jetty. But they were too small to take home, so we'd thrown them back, along with the occasional rock cod whose greediness had overcome its natural ability to strip off the bait without getting hooked.

We'd been out since before dawn, so by eight o'clock, without any decent-sized fish about, we were ready to pack up when my fluoro-orange float suddenly ducked under the water and the line from the rod went taut. It didn't feel like a fish strike, though – more like the hook had got caught up with a big bunch of seaweed. But there wasn't any weed out where my float had been – and that orange flash was six feet down and heading further underwater. The line was also playing out, but much more slowly than it would if I had a big fish on.

I started to reel in and carefully walked the three metres or so to the end of the jetty, because I thought I might be able to see what I'd hooked up. Whatever was on the end of the line was very heavy, because after only a few turns of the reel the tip of the rod was bent right over and I thought the line would snap at any moment.

Then I saw it. A huge, wriggling brown shape in the water. A thing with a round body that was easily a metre in diameter, surrounded by floating tentacles that writhed around out another metre and a half.

It was the biggest octopus I'd ever seen. It was huge!

I screamed at Dad to come and have a look and help me get it in, though as soon as I'd said that, I wondered if it was a good idea. What would it be like to have a humungous octopus on the jetty, lashing out with its tentacles?

Dad came over to take a look. He was impressed by the size of it, as were a couple of other fishermen who heard the commotion and came over from the rocks at the foot of the jetty.

All of them agreed that there was no way that we could get the octopus ashore, and Dad told me that even if we could somehow reel it in, we should let it go.

Reluctantly, I cut the line. It didn't seem to make much difference to the octopus. It drifted in closer, under the jetty. I started to wonder if it might climb up one of the piers. Maybe it was annoyed, and it was going to try and get me...

Then it suddenly convulsed, all the tentacles whipping around, and it headed out to sea again. It wasn't really moving that quickly, but after its simple drifting motion, it seemed fast. I watched it till it entered the darker band of blue sea, and was lost to sight.

I have no photographs to remind me, and I'm not known to have the best memory in town, but the image of that writhing, wriggling thing in the blue-green water is as clear to me now as if it happened last week, not thirty-two years ago, and once again I remember the day I caught a giant octopus.

Jamie Oliver

MINI PIZZAS

I love making these little pizzas with my kids. If you prefer, you can try making the base with wholemeal flour as it's a healthier option. There are all sorts of toppings you can do – the one I'm giving you here is really basic and you should all be able to make it easily. These pizzas are great for packed lunches as they can be eaten cold. They can also be made bigger if you want – see what takes your fancy.

Makes about 12

340g self-raising flour
a pinch of salt
85g butter
8 tablespoons milk
2 tablespoons olive oil

for the topping:
6 tomatoes, sliced
250ml passata
2 150g balls of mozzarella, torn or sliced
a small bunch of fresh basil leaves
100g good melting cheese like Cheddar or fontina, grated

Preheat the oven to 200°C/ 400°F/ gas 6.

Sift the flour and salt into a bowl and rub in the butter until the mixture resembles fine breadcrumbs, or you could ask your mum or dad to help you whiz the mixture in a food processor. Add the milk and olive oil and mix again until you have a soft dough.

Tear off a golf ball-sized piece of dough and roll it out until you have a rough circle shape, about ½ cm thick. Lay the rolled out pieces of dough side by side on a greased and floured baking tray, cover each with a thin layer of passata and a slice of tomato. Top with a small piece of mozzarella, a basil leaf and a sprinkling of cheese. Bake for 15–20 minutes until the base is golden and the cheese has melted.

Louise Rennison

GEORGIA NICOLSON'S GUIDE TO
A SUMMER OF LUUURRVE

As you know, during the hot summer months we will all be prancing about the Costa del Fiasco in the nearly nuddy-pants. Because I love you all so much, I have taken time off from heavy plucking to give you my top tips.

A suggestion of the rampant orang-utan gene can spoil a lovely holiday. Pluck for England so that you do not have just the one eyebrow right across your forehead.

Secondly, it is vair important to check the back of your legs too - you don't want a baboon-in-a-swimming-cosy-effect, rear-wise.

Don't fiddle about with your thong bikini, fishing it out of your bum-oley etc. It's not that boys don't like this. They do. A lot. But it lacks sophisticosity.

Make-up-wise, lighten up, man! It's summer! Go natural. Having said that, don't go mad - natural doesn't mean really really plain. So just a hint of foundation, lippy, lip-gloss, mascara, touch of eye shadow, eye liner and nail polish.

Always remember to remove your sunglasses before snogging - to avoid being locked in shade-to-shade combat with your snoggee. (Also, he might be concealing spaggy-eye syndrome behind his shades.)

The golden rule for holiday romance is this: have a LOT. Sound the Cosmic Horn! If you do accidentally acquire a Pizza-a-gogo land boyfriend, just remember this: dump him when you leave. Pedro's obsession with hair gel and novelty shorts will not be so much fun in your living room.

Travel wisely and take a book that is full of wisdomosity, and also one that you can keep laughing at to annoy your parents while they admire the view. That is, one of mine.

That's it. Have a megafab summer, everybody! I love you. I do. I know I don't know you, but now you're being picky. But I still love you.

Georgia

XXX

THE SAMUEL Z GREST ADVENTURES

Darren Shan

TRANSYLVANIA TREK: THE MYSTERY BEGINS

As soon as the phone rang, I knew I was in trouble. I always know when trouble's brewing, because the blue rat who lives inside my head starts to shiver with fear. When the phone rang he shivered so much that my eyeballs juggled up and down.

"What's wrong?" I asked, picking up the phone and shaking my head to stop the blue rat from shivering. I listened carefully.

It was Moss Biskin, who I knew from when I had to kill a zombie who was eating kids in Brussels. Moss said he was in Transylvania, looking for vampires (Moss is always looking for something or other), and he'd found...

The phone went dead before he could finish. "Moss?" I asked, giving it a shake in case it was only faulty wiring. There was no answer. "This is bad," I said to the blue rat.

"Tell me about it!" he squeaked. "I think you should pretend you never got that phone call."

"You know I can't do that," I said.

"I know," the blue rat sighed, then crawled out my left ear and slid down my shoulder to the floor. "Sorry, Sam, but I can't go with you this time. It's too dangerous. I don't think you'll come back." Then he ran away down a hole. I didn't blame him. I knew he had a wife and forty-six ratlings to think about.

On the Wings of Danger

I knew it was going to be a rocky flight when I saw the stewardesses wearing parachutes. They pretended it was just for a test, but I knew better. When the plane started shaking halfway to Transylvania, and they jumped out the door, leaving me and the other passengers behind, I wasn't the least bit surprised.

"Calm down!" I shouted when everyone started screaming. "I'll take care of this. Sit down and don't say anything. And don't move about, in case you rock the plane too much."

When everyone was sitting, I ran to the front of the plane and busted down the cockpit door. There was a creature inside who would have scared a lesser mortal to death. He was huge, with two big wings and dark green fangs. I didn't know who he was, but there was something familiar about him.

"Let's see you get out of this one, Grest!" the creature grunted, ripping off the plane's steering wheel and throwing it at me. I ducked out of the way of the wheel, but when I stood up again the creature had leapt through the window and went flying away with his wings.

If the blue rat was with me, I could have sent him down the hole left by the steering wheel and he could have put the wires back together and flown the plane from in there. But I was all alone. Of course, I could have jumped out and used the mini parachute I always carry in the heel of my left shoe, but there were the other passengers to think about. So I ripped off the entire panel of buttons and levers, and grabbed the wires myself. It wasn't easy, but I managed to land the plane in a very big pond just down the road from Dracula's castle. When I'd got everyone else out, the plane sank and I jumped ashore.

I had arrived in Transylvania!!!

Count Dracula, I presume?

Dracula's castle had been abandoned for years, but I wasn't fooled. I knew the vampire was there. Who else could have caused the brave and daring Moss Biskin so much fear? Going up the mountain, I tried to get to the castle before the sun set, but I'd forgotten to put my watch forwards, so I got the time wrong, and the sun sank down behind the castle just as I got to the big front door.

I stood there for ages, not sure what to do next. I knew I should run away until morning, when the sun came back up. But Moss Biskin was in danger and needed my help. So even though I knew I was maybe signing my own death warrant, I pushed the door open and went in.

There were cobwebs all over the place, big and huge, white and sticky. I didn't see the spiders, but I could hear them rubbing their legs together and hissing as I went past.

"We meet again!" the creature from the plane shouted, leaping out behind me when I got to a tall balcony. He locked his arms around me. "Now I'll kill you at last, for murdering my brother!"

Suddenly it all clicked and I knew why he looked familiar. I'd killed his brother, the Monster from Mongolia, a couple of months before. "You won't kill me, any more than your brother did," I laughed, breaking his hold on me. I grabbed him by his fangs and threw him over the edge of the balcony.

"Noooooo!" he screamed as he fell, but it was no good. He landed hard on the floor and broke his back, then the spiders came down and ate him alive while he was screaming. It was most horrible and ghastly — but heck, he deserved it!

"Vell done, Meester Grest," Dracula said. Turning quickly, I saw the vampire standing in front of me, smiling nastily. "You are a vorthy opponent. Such a peety I have to kill you." Saying that, he pressed a switch and the floor beneath me disappeared. I dropped into a pit full of poisonous cobra snakes.

A Narrow Escape

I would have been a goner, except I know how to charm snakes and always carry a flute in my bag. Pulling it out, I started to play and soon all the snakes were asleep. Dracula saw this and cursed. He threw big rocks down on me, trying to squash me, but all he did was wake and anger the cobras, who slithered up and attacked him. He ran away from them, screaming as they bit his legs and bum. I laughed and set off after him.

That was when my real enemy leaped forward and showed himself.

The True Face of Evil

I realised too late that Dracula was only a decoy. He wasn't what Moss Biskin had phoned to tell me about. It was a werewolf who was killing all the people. A giant, hairy werewolf, with sword-like claws and long jagged teeth. He dragged me to the ground while I was still laughing at Dracula being bitten by the snakes. I tried to push him off but he was too strong.

The werewolf howled in my face. I'm not afraid of anything in this world – except werewolves! I can't stand them! Trying hard not to cry, I punched the werewolf and ran away, but he was too quick. He caught me. Rolling me over, he clawed a big hole in my belly, then stuck his jaws down to suck my guts out. I was in *big* trouble. I couldn't escape. Was this to be the grisly end of the intrepid Samuel Z Grest?!?

Rescued from the Jaws of Defeat

No, it wasn't! At the last minute, as the werewolf started to suck, something jumped on his shoulder and bit his ears. He screamed and fell away from me. Sitting up, I saw the last thing in the world I had expected to see – the blue rat who lives inside my head!

"Hello, Sam," he said, smiling. "You didn't think I'd really let you come here by yourself, did you? I've been following you all along, waiting for the werewolf to make his move."

"Have you killed him?" I asked, because the werewolf was lying very still now on the floor.

"No," the blue rat said. "I put special ointment on my teeth when I bit him. It will make him better."

I watched as the werewolf's hairs began to vanish. After a while, he turned back into a human and I could barely believe it when I saw who he was.

"Moss Biskin!" I shouted happily, helping him sit back up.

"What's happening?" Moss Biskin asked, shaking his head stupidly. The blue rat and I laughed at his funny expression, then took him down the mountain, dragged up the plane from the bottom of the pond, and flew back home, where we told Moss Biskin all about it over three cups of tea and a plate of warm rat biscuits.

BRIDE OF SAM GREST:
BEAUTY ENTERS MY LIFE

I was playing chess with my best friend, Moss Biskin, and the blue rat who lives inside my head. Moss was in the middle of telling me about a cannibal he'd defeated in the Abalon Jungle when the door to my office burst open and the most beautiful girl I'd ever seen entered, screaming, her eyes wild with terror.

"Help!" she yelled. "It's after me! It's going to eat me! It…"

Before she could say any more, she fainted, and I had to jump forward quickly to catch her before she hit the floor.

A Tale of Horror

Her name was Demonia. She had a lovely face, long hair and slim hands. Her feet were big, but that was OK – I've always fancied girls with big feet.

"Who do you think she is?" the blue rat asked. He was shivering, the way he always does at the start of a dangerous case.

"I don't know," I said.

"I don't trust her," Moss Biskin grunted.

"Shut up!" I snapped, brushing her hair from her face, gazing at her closed eyelids and her gently parted lips as she breathed lightly, still asleep. (I knew her name because I'd read it on the label inside her jacket when I'd taken it off and hung it up.)

Eventually Demonia awoke. "Where am I?" she gasped, staring around, frightened.

"It's OK," I told her. "You're safe. I'm Sam Grest."

She smiled when she heard that. "Thank heavens!" she cried. "I was trying to get here when the monster attacked."

"Monster?!?" Moss Biskin, the rat and I shouted together, alarmed but excited — it had been almost a month since we'd last had a scrap with a really nasty monster.

Over a cup of tea and a plate of warm rat biscuits, Demonia told us about the monster that had attacked her, her brother and two of their friends. It was a purple-skinned, fat creature, which dressed in a white suit and drank the blood of its victims. It had killed her two friends and kidnapped her brother. It said it would eat Demonia's brother unless Demonia married it.

"Don't worry!" I interrupted hotly. "I won't let that happen!"

"Thank you, Mr Grest," Demonia said, kissing me to show how grateful she was.

"Please," I muttered, blushing madly, "call me Sam."

In Hot Pursuit

I wanted to leave with Demonia straight away, but Moss and the blue rat were less than enthusiastic. "There's something wrong about her," the blue rat squeaked.

"I don't think she told us the whole truth," Moss Biskin added.

"You two are just jealous," I replied, "because I'm the only one she kissed. You can stay here and mind the office – I'll go with her by myself!"

Moss and the blue rat tried to talk me out of it, but I wouldn't listen, and soon I'd left with Demonia in search of her brother. She kissed me again when we were alone, and said she was falling in love with me. I hadn't felt as happy since I'd cut off the head of a murdering ogre on the banks of the Zalabu river!

The last time Demonia saw the purple monster, it had been heading for the cliffs of Dead Man's Munch. I knew those cliffs well – they were one of the few places I'd gone out of my way to avoid in the past, knowing how deadly they are. I almost went back to get Moss Biskin and the blue rat – I was scared – but Demonia hugged me tight and kissed me a third time, and after that nothing in the world frightened me, so off we set!

On the Cliffs

Strong winds howled around the cliffs of Dead Man's Munch. The cliffs were some of the tallest in the world, and the ground at the bottom was rough and sharp – if we fell, it would be the end of us! Demonia and I crept along the edge of the cliffs, trying to avoid the hands of dead people, which stuck out of the rocks and swiped at us as we walked past, trying to knock us off. We were doing quite a good job of it, and were almost at the end of the cliffs, when a hand struck me hard in the back. I teetered on the edge a moment, but then gravity grabbed me and I toppled over — and fell to what seemed a certain, grisly death!

A Narrow Escape

I would have been a goner, except in the nick of time I remembered the mini parachute I keep in the heel of my left shoe. I ripped the shoe off, held it above my head and tapped three times on the heel. To my intense relief, the heel slid open and the parachute blossomed out. I landed a few seconds later, harder than I would have wished — but alive!

As I was sitting up, tucking the parachute back into the heel of my shoe, Demonia appeared. "You're alive!" she exclaimed.

"It'll take more than a simple fall to kill Sam Grest," I chuckled, then frowned. "How did *you* get down here?"

Demonia smiled crookedly. "I climbed down," she said. "I was so worried about you, I didn't stop to consider my own safety."

I couldn't see how she'd done it — the cliffs were so sheer, I'd have said they were impossible to climb. But then she kissed me again and I stopped worrying. Slipping my shoe back on, I clambered to my feet and we went looking for Demonia's brother.

Where Evil Dwells!

After a short search, we discovered a tunnel underneath the cliffs of Dead Man's Munch. I zipped out the torch I always carry, flicked it on, and we advanced. Demonia was breathing heavily. I assumed it was with fear, so I gave her a hug to cheer her up. She felt bigger than she'd been before, and wider, but I couldn't see very well, so I put it down to my imagination.

The tunnel led to a huge cave full of stalactites and stalagmites. There was a platform at the centre of the cave. On it was a slab. On the slab lay the rotting corpses of two monsters. Next to the slab stood a fat, purple-skinned man with red eyes and fingernails. He was giggling uncontrollably.

"Who are you?" I shouted. "Where's Demonia's brother?"

"My brother's on the slab — and so's my other brother," Demonia said behind me, and her voice was much lower and thicker than it had been. Turning to look at her, I got the shock of my life — she'd changed into a monster!

Revelations

"What's going on?" I roared, stumbling away from the monster.

"*Revenge* is what's going on!" Demonia sneered. She was huge now, with big red wings and dark green fangs. Her ears were pointy and her eyes were sharp like a demon's. "You killed my brothers, so now I'm here to kill you!"

All of a sudden, I understood what was happening. "Your brother was the Monster from Mongolia!" I gasped. I'd killed him a long time ago. His brother had tried to return the favour in Transylvania several months later, and I'd killed him too. I now knew there'd been a third member of the M.F.M. family – a sister!

"You can go now, Murlough," Demonia said to the purple-skinned creature on the platform. "Thanks for the help."

"No problem, dear lady," Murlough gurgled in reply, then left by the rear exit.

"Now for you!" Demonia hissed, creeping towards me on five hairy legs. "I thought I'd killed you when I pushed you over the edge of the cliff, but when I flew down after you, I found you'd survived. You got lucky that time, but your luck ends here!"

So it hadn't been one of the hands of the dead that knocked me over – Demonia did it!

"Stop!" I warned her. "Don't make me kill you like I killed your brothers!"

"You can't kill me!" she jeered. "When I was in disguise and kissed you, I was wearing magical lipstick. That's why you fell in love with me, and that's why you won't be able to harm me!"

To my horror, I realised she was telling the truth – when I tried to raise a hand to fight her, it wouldn't move! I was completely powerless – and about to die!

Sweet Timing

Demonia was almost upon me, claws exposed, fangs dripping with green drool. "I'll kill you slowly!" she croaked. "And I'll eat you. And when I'm finished, I'll squat over a toilet and—"

"Not so fast!" someone shouted behind her.

Spinning, the monster found herself faced with a grim Moss Biskin and a glowering blue rat. "What are you doing here?" Demonia screeched.

"We followed you," Moss Biskin said. "We guessed what you were up to."

"You're fools if you think you can kill me," Demonia snarled.

"We don't intend to," the blue rat said, then raced between the monster's five legs and handed me a damp handkerchief. "Use it quick!" he told me. "We smeared it with the antidote to her lipstick."

Demonia screamed when she heard that and darted towards me. But I was quicker than the monster. I wiped my lips clean with one swift sweep, pulled an axe out of my rucksack, and cut her head off just as she was about to devour me.

"Well," Moss said, stepping up beside me, "that was a close one!"

"Yes," I sighed, glad to be alive, but sad at the same time.

"Never mind," the blue rat said, crawling back inside my ear to its home. "You'll fall in love again. Plenty more fish in the sea."

"Let's just hope there aren't plenty more Monsters from Mongolia!" Moss Biskin laughed. And after a brief reflective pause, I turned my back on the dead beast, bid farewell to the memory of the only girl I'd ever loved, slung an arm around Moss Biskin's shoulder — and I laughed too.

THE END

THE GIRL IN THE TOWER

Jonathan Stroud

A writer sat in an attic; he heard the rain on the roof tiles and the mice running behind the wall. He drummed his fingers on the paper laid out on the desk, leaving little pit-a-pat ink marks like horses' hooves on the empty page. At last, tiring of this, he craned his neck back as far as it would go, until he was staring straight up at the skylight overhead. Grey clouds scudded past, driven by the same wind that blew in under his locked door and made the base of his back ache.

A pen was lying on the table. He picked it up and

took off the cap, making a little metallic squeak. He stood the cap up on its end and watched it fall down, tried balancing it once more, failed, and at last stuck it out horizontally from a squodge of blu-tak on the lip of the desk.

Then he began to write, and the following words came naturally to him:

Once there was a writer with a melancholy heart. He

put down his pen for a moment and scratched under his arm. Then, his mind wandering, he drew a rude picture in the margin of the paper, of a sort he had drawn many times before. It didn't give him the guilty thrill he had experienced when he had first drawn something like it, years ago in an old school text book, and when he looked again at the sentence he had written, it too seemed wrong – tired somehow, as if it had been used before – so he scrubbed it out with a single line and started again.

Once upon a time there was a girl who loved to write. She was very beautiful, and as she came of age, many rich lords sought her hand in marriage. But she rejected every one of them, preferring to sit at her desk with her pen in hand, and dream. Some days, a dozen stories flowed from her, but at other times the inspiration was slow to come. On one such afternoon, she sat at her desk staring sadly at the empty page. Then

he stopped writing again and wrinkled his brow at the sheet that now seemed quite full, what with his passage, the false start, the rude picture and the little mass of fingermarks lightly covering the lowest third. Aimlessly, he drew little stick trunks under each spot of inky foliage, until a dense forest spread out across the paper. There was a gap, or glade, in the centre of the fingerprint forest. With a pen he drew a couple of quick strokes, a triangle above, a tiny rectangle within... Now a tower stood in the forest, with a single window looking out upon the trees.

Then he returned to his paragraph, and

she got up from her chair and walked over to the long window that looked out upon the olive-dark canopy of the forest. Sheets of rain fell in waves; overhead the sky was a slab of grey, save for a thick white slash on the horizon, beyond the rain.

She ran her hands through her long dark hair, rotating her head slightly, ridding herself of the aches that, by way of a subtle draught, had settled on her that afternoon.

"No one will come here," she said aloud. "The forest is too wide and its dangers are too terrible. I shall sit in this room for ever." A gust of rain lashed against the window, and throughout its dim, dry innards of oak and brick, its echoing stairs and hidden spaces, the age-old tower shuddered.

The writer went back to her chair. Along with the desk and pen, her inks and papers, it was the only possession the prince had allowed her. His soldiers had carried it across the forest, swords drawn against the creatures watching from the dark, then hauled it up a thousand steps to the attic room. Made of red leather, with brass studs on the seams, it now had cracks from heavy usage on the armrests and the seat.

She eased herself down and the leather creaked in muffled protest.

The writer rewarded himself with a smile. He stretched his arms above and behind his head and heard the chair's wooden back creak almost in unison with his creation's. Poor girl! Trapped like a bird in a cage. Well, there she would remain unless he chose to let her out. His thoughts dwelt a moment on her long dark hair, her pensive beauty... At this, the rude picture caught his eye again. This time its presence annoyed him; he scrubbed it out till it was hidden under a thick cloud of cross-hatching. Irritably he glanced about his mean little room. The light was poor and shadows clustered in the eaves. The afternoon was waning.

Picking up her pen once more, the girl's mind drifted: she recalled the prince's stammering proposal, his hundred gifts – the gold, the silken dresses, the birds of paradise in their silver cage. She recalled his numb bewilderment at her answer, his pale face blotching with fury, his last words hissed as she was led away: "If writing is your heart's desire, you shall have that pleasure eternally. I shall see that you are never again disturbed."

The prince's promise was fulfilled. The door to the staircase was locked and the key taken away. Her cries were muffled behind the thick glass of the window at the top of the tower, and there was no one in the forest to hear should she have broken it. Then the wind and rain would only have come in and drenched her, and she would have died of cold.

The writer shivered and rubbed his neck. Like a fool he had forgotten to buy a bulb for the attic's single light, and now it was getting hard to see: he had to squint at the page to make it out. He bit the end of the pen, leaving little tooth marks in the plastic.

The paper on her desk was empty, except for little blue specks where her inky fingertips had rested earlier that afternoon. She stared at them, trying to kick-start her imagination.

But nothing came into her head except remembered dapples on her horses' flanks, the patterns of hoof-prints on wet turf and, unbidden, the memory of the air outside.

"Without a companion," she whispered, "I shall surely die."

He was bent over his page, scribbling ever faster. Evening had come; the sky was darkening. His form grew dimmer by the word.

The writer tapped her pen against her lips. Her mouth tightened; strong creases at the corners gave it a newly stubborn look. Anger burned in her eyes.

"I shall defy him!" she said loudly. "I shall not die, and nor will I be alone. Here and now, I shall create a companion for myself."

He was only a blurred form in the twilight now, silent save for the scratching of his pen.

"Let's see," she said. "Who shall we have? Perhaps—"

She set her pen to the paper.

A writer

leaped up from his chair, threw his pen down. She could stop right there! But darkness filled the room and a loud chittering came from behind the wall. Rain lashed against the skylight and it was black outside. He stretched out a hand... Ah! – he could no longer see himself, and nor could he see to write...

Where was the pen? He leaned towards the desk – ow! – jabbing himself on the pen cap still sticking out from the lip. Back and forth over the desktop he ran his fingers. They closed on the pen. He seated himself. The chair creaked. Breathing heavily, he squinted down where his papers had once been.

It was no good. It was too dark. He could not see where he had left off. In desperation he snatched at the sheets of paper, scattering them across the desk. He seized one at random and held the pen above it. Quickly then, what could he write? Anything would do. He waited. Nothing came to him. His mind was a blank.

His fingers relaxed. He let the pen fall. The blackness swallowed him.

She set her pen to the paper.

A writer sat in an attic; she

paused and looked at the last word she had written. Should her companion perhaps be a man? Thunder rolled; away through the window lightning crackled above the forest, illuminating distant treetops. She shook her head. No. It had been a man who had imprisoned her here in the desolate tower. She wanted nothing more to do with men! The person she created would be a woman, someone who understood her love of words, who would identify with her situation. She smiled as she began to write again. It all seemed simple now. Her companion would be

A writer sat in an attic; she heard the rain on the roof tiles and the mice running behind the wall. She drummed her fingers on the paper laid out on the desk, leaving little pit-a-pat ink marks like horses' hooves on the empty page…

SIR KILFAY AND THE NANO-SPIES

Eleanor Updale

My Dear Sam,

I think it's time I told you this. How I am responsible for one of the most infuriating things in your life. I didn't mean to do it. It seemed like a good idea at the time, all those years ago, in the early 1990s, when I was eleven. You'd think one of the grown ups would have foreseen what would happen. Maybe they did, and they went ahead anyway. I can't ask my parents. They're dead, and everyone else involved would just deny it ever happened. There's just me. I'm the only one outside the system who knows about it. Perhaps the only one who can put it right.

I suppose I had a strange childhood, though my sister and I didn't think so. It was all we'd ever known, trailing round the world from one British embassy to another, staying in each country for about three years or so. Mum said we were lucky that the posting to Komque had come up. There was an international school there, and we could live with our parents, instead of being sent to boarding schools in England. It was fun, mixing with friends of all nationalities, and playing in the sunshine all year long.

But Charlotte and I both knew something strange was going on. When Mum was talking to the other diplomatic wives she would sometimes drop her voice, look sideways at us and say "pas devant", which we knew was French for "not in front", as in "not in front of the children". Then she'd change the subject to something really stupid like flower arranging or recipes, and we sensed that we were missing out on a juicy titbit. But occasionally things slipped though; and we became obsessed with one name in particular, whispered with a hint of mystery in the drawing room or down the phone. That name was "Sir Kilfay".

There were lots of 'Sirs' in our lives, from Sir Digby Forrest-Wilson, the Ambassador, to the Foreign Secretary Sir Quentin Lovatt, who had terrible B.O. and bad breath, though no one had the courage to tell him. But the thing about Sir Kilfay was that we never met him, even though Mum was always mentioning him. Time and again I overheard her say, "Of course, Peter will never be promoted to his true level because of Sir Kilfay." or "We have to be careful," dropping her voice to add "You know... bearing in mind Sir Kilfay." And when the Honours List came out at New Year, Charlotte heard her tell one of her friends, "It's hard not to be jealous of Martin's OBE. Peter will never get one." and Mum sighed, adding "Sir Kilfay, I'm afraid."

But who was Sir Kilfay? We decided that he must be someone important back at the Foreign Office in London, who had something against our father. That was why Dad was stuck in what sounded like a pretty boring job, sorting out visas for people who wanted to visit Britain. When he came home in the evenings, Mum would say. "How was your day, Darling?" And every night, Dad would reply, "Oh you know – the usual." We felt sorry for him.

Charlotte and I despised Sir Kilfay. We decided to write and tell him to stop picking on Dad, but we couldn't get his address. We tried looking him up in the Diplomatic List, but without his surname, it was hopeless.

"Why don't we just ask Mum or Dad?" I said, as Charlotte put the book back.

"Don't be silly, Jonathan," she whispered. "You've seen how Mum gets when she talks about him, especially when we're around. We're not supposed to know about him. It's something secret. Something bad."

"It's a pretty silly name, 'Kilfay'," I said. "I've never heard it before."

"Odd," said Charlotte. "But he wouldn't be the only one whose parents had a rush of blood to the head in the maternity ward. Look at this," she said, taking another book off the shelf, "*Despotism in Disguise* by Sir Dingle Foot. Or this: *Eastern Approaches* by Sir Fitzroy Maclean. Anyway. It's not his name that's important. It's the effect he's having on us all. It's obvious that Mum blames him for holding Dad back, and that he's even putting Dad in some sort of danger. We'll just have to keep our ears open in case anyone else mentions him."

"But they never do, do they?" I said. "It's only Mum. I've never heard Dad say a word about him."

"Dad never discusses work at all, you know that," said Charlotte. "Poor man. It must be so dreary for him. He can't bear to talk about it. There's no point asking him."

And yet it was Dad who finally, inadvertently, revealed the secret. He used to take me swimming every Saturday, driving across the city in the big Volvo to an open-air pool down near the beach. It was special time together. Dad always took the same peculiar route, diverting down a series of side streets, instead of using the main road. And I'd noticed that he always slowed down at the same places, paying special attention to the pedestrians. Two weeks running he followed a young man, and when that man went into a house, Dad muttered the house number, "27", to himself. The next week I watched the man, and he went into a different house. Dad said nothing. I couldn't help myself.

"29," I said. "He went into 29 this week. Not 27."

Dad gripped the steering wheel very hard. He accelerated away, and drove down to the seafront, parking well away from other cars. "Come on," he said, getting out and walking across the beach towards the water, where no one could overhear our conversation. "So you know," he said. "I thought so. You've worked it out."

"Worked what out?"

"You know what I really do, don't you? Why I'm here."

I didn't know how to react. It was beginning to dawn on me that Dad's job involved something more than sorting through visa applications and interviewing would-be immigrants to Britain.

Dad saved me from replying. "You know what 'intelligence' is, don't you?" he asked, staring out towards the waves. "I don't mean the kind they talk about at school."

"You mean spying," I said.

"Well, we don't like to call it that," said Dad, "but intelligence is what I'm involved in. I have to collect information. Watch certain people, and so on."

"That's why you've been following the man at number 27?" I asked.

"Yes, and I should have been more careful. I shouldn't have let you see what was going on. Anyway, that man's not so very important. But there are others here plotting against Britain. We think they may be sending arms to terrorists in Northern Ireland. I have to keep an eye on suspects, to wait for them to put a foot wrong so that we can stop them killing people back home. Now that you know, I must beg you to be discreet. I don't want you boasting about this to your schoolmates. This work is not glamorous, but it could be dangerous for all of us if the wrong people find out what I really do. Keep it under your hat, OK?"

I said of course I would, but I couldn't resist one more question. It seemed the right time to ask. "Dad, is all this something to do with Sir Kilfay?"

Dad looked puzzled. "Who?"

"Sir Kilfay. I've overheard Mum talking about him. Charlotte and I both have. We know he's put you in danger. We know he's holding back your career."

There was a long pause. Then the mystification on Dad's face turned into a smile. "Sir Kilfay," he said. "Sir Kilfay..." Then he laughed. "It's not Sir Kilfay, silly. It's French. Your mother's been speaking French to hide something from you. It's 'ce qu'il fait'."

"What does that mean?"

"Ce qu'il fait? It means 'what he does'."

"So when Mum says you won't get an OBE because of 'ce qu'il fait'..."

"Does she really? Dad smiled to himself. I think he was surprised to discover that Mum cared about titles and honours. "Well, what she means is that my work can't be recognised publicly because of what I do." He put his arm round my shoulder. It felt odd. It was ages since he'd hugged me or anything like that. I'd missed the old closeness. Perhaps he had too. He ruffled up my hair. "Jonboy," he said, using his old pet name for me. "Now that you know, maybe the two of us can speak a little more freely, in private. I've never liked having a secret from my own son. I can't go into details, of course, but perhaps we can be a bit more grown up when we are alone together."

It felt good to be trusted by Dad. And he liked it too. The Saturday morning swims turned into walks along the beach, with him dropping hints, and going just a little too far letting me into his world. After he'd parked the car, he'd say, "Right Jonboy, let's go and see Sir Kilfay!" – revelling in the confusion that must have caused any enemy agents listening in.

It was as if he was trying to impress me. He told me about the gadgets he used as part of his spying work. He knew I loved new technology. So in a way he was showing off one Saturday when he told me about a top-secret tracking device that was being developed. It was a transmitter so tiny that the target would never know it had been planted on his clothes. "It's what they call 'nano-technology'," said Dad. "The whole thing is a fraction of the size of a grain of rice. The circuits inside it have to be manufactured under microscopes. And here's the good news, Jonboy. We've been chosen to do the first trials, here in Komque. If I could plant transmitters on suspects I wouldn't have to follow them round in our lumbering old car with its diplomatic plates. We'd know where they were, who they met, how long they spent together. We'd know exactly who to..."

"Eliminate?" I asked.

He coughed. "Report to the authorities," he said, stiffly.

I had gone too far. It was not my place to ask what use Dad made of his information. I tried to sound boyish and enthusiastic again. "Have you got one of these trackers? Can I have a look?"

"If I did have, you wouldn't be able to see it. They're that small," laughed Dad. "That's one of the problems actually. You can plant the transmitters by just brushing against someone, but they are so minute that they drop off fabric easily, and of course if the target takes off his clothes, we've lost him. The boffins back in England are trying to find some sort of fixative. Maybe something that will attach to human skin and not wash off in the bath. It's a real challenge."

Some people were coming the other way, and we had to stop talking. We never discussed spying in the car, just in case it was bugged, and so the subject was long dropped when we got home, to find Mum dragging a fine comb through Charlotte's wet hair.

"I had a call from George's mother," she said.

I hoped she was going to tell me I could go to watch a hockey match with my friend from school, but it was bad news. "George and Bertie have both got head lice. They must have picked them up when they went home to London at Half Term. You'll have to be checked I'm afraid. These things spread like wildfire. Charlotte seems clear so far."

"Head lice!" said dad, horrified. In those days nits

weren't as common as they are now, and the idea of his children being infested filled him with shame and dread. "How appallingly Victorian."

On the Monday, they gave out a leaflet at school. It told you all about the lifecycle of the louse, and how it attached its eggs to your hair with a special glue. That set me thinking. And that's how I came up with my idea. The idea that has led to so much trouble over the years. I never really thought that Dad would take it seriously, let alone pass it on to the government scientists back in Britain. But he did, and they followed it up. Within weeks, secret laboratories were working on a project to implant the new nano-transmitters into head lice, just where their eggs come out. The idea was that the chip would be ejected from the louse's body in a globule of natural head louse adhesive, bonding the transmitter to the hair alongside the eggs. They called the tiny creatures delivering the revolutionary spyware "nano-spies".

Even before the research programme, parents were beginning to discover how difficult it could be to remove lice and their eggs from children's heads. It was even worse after selective breeding produced lice with stronger legs to hold on to hair, and a more powerful glue to cement their eggs in place. Eventually the scientists were convinced they had developed a louse that could support a transmitter, and a device that looked just like an egg. It could survive any amount of shampooing, brushing or combing. The companies that made the special nit lotion were even persuaded by the government to stop trying to develop more effective formulations. (Actually, that bit wasn't very hard. It suited them to keep the lice in business. After all, if nits disappeared, no one would want to buy their products again.)

And that's how it happened. That's why head lice were allowed to develop into one of the most successful species on earth.

But back at the beginning, it just seemed clever. Dad was really excited about being at the heart of the project, and he volunteered Charlotte and me to deliver the first, experimental bugs. We were infested with the special lice, and instructed to find a way of "accidentally" making our heads come into contact with our school friends' hair. Soon they had infected their parents, and our embassy knew just where diplomats from the French, Italian, and American embassies were at all times. Of course, they weren't the real targets, and getting the lice into the families of terrorist suspects amongst the local population took more work. There were chance encounters at sports arenas, in shopping centres and cinemas. Dad started coming home from work with a smile on his face. There were arrests. On Saturdays we drove to the sea without the old detours.

But no one had thought to develop a way to stop the nano-spies laying normal eggs alongside the transmitters. Those eggs hatched into normal lice, but stronger and stickier than ever. Every night each louse produced thousands more. Soon the whole town was itching, and complaining that the "little visitors" seemed to have become resistant to the chemicals designed to eradicate them. And people travelled. The diplomats' children took lice all over the world. By the end of the century the little monsters were causing tears and shouting in almost every household across the globe as weary parents struggled to pull nit combs through tangled mats before bedtime. Drug companies made fortunes selling their inadequate remedies. And no one could understand why the human race couldn't defeat a creature the size of a pinhead.

I knew of course. But I had promised my father I wouldn't tell. He warned me that our whole family would be at risk if our enemies ever found out how we had tracked down some of their most important operatives. But now my parents are dead. Dad never did get his OBE. Just as Mum predicted, "Sir Kilfay" saw to that. I hope the car crash that killed them really was an accident. I wish Charlotte hadn't accepted a lift from them that day. Now I'm the only one left. The only one who knows the truth.

That's why I'm writing this now. I may not live long. For as long as I do, I am going to devote myself to putting right some of the damage I have caused. I don't care whether the security services are still using nano-spies. Maybe they are. Maybe our enemies have them. I saw our own Prime Minister scratching his head on television only the other day. Perhaps nano-spies as I knew them are old technology now. These days they may be able to read minds as well as just broadcast locations. But even if they are still used, I think the world has suffered enough. I've seen you and your sister squirming and crying as your mother tries to clean your heads with those foul-smelling potions.

So I'm going to do something about it. On my own, in my garden shed. I'm going to find a chemical to dissolve the glue that sticks the nits to hair. And I'm going to sell it for a fraction of the price of the official remedies. Then the lice and their eggs can all be washed down the plughole and children everywhere can enjoy the life I led until I was eleven – a life without itching, choking and pain. But I'll have to work in secret. If the government and the drug companies find out, they might send me the way of the rest of my family. We must never speak of the project, Sam. Not openly, of course.

Just think of it as "what I do" – "ce que je fais" or "Sir Kerr Gervais", a cousin of our old friend, Sir Kilfay, and a distant relative of

Your loving godfather,

Jonathan

About the contributors

Jessica Adams is the author of two books for children — *Amazing You Astrology* and *Amazing You Psychic Powers*. She has worked on all the anthologies in aid of War Child and is a columnist at *Vogue* and *The Australian Women's Weekly* and a Contributing Editor at *Cosmopolitan, UK*.

Meg Cabot is the author of over forty books for both adults and teens, many of which have been bestsellers, most notably The *Princess Diaries* series, which is currently being published in over 37 countries, has sold over five million copies worldwide, and was made into two hit movies by Disney. In addition, Meg wrote *the Mediator* and *1-800-Where-R-You?* series (on which the television series, *Missing*, was based), two All-American Girl books, *Teen Idol*, *Avalon High*, *How to Be Popular*, many historical romance novels under a pen name she still hopes her grandma never finds out about, a series of novels written entirely in email format (*Boy Next Door, Boy Meets Girl,* and *Every Boy's Got One*), a mystery series (*Size 12 Is Not Fat / Size 14 Is Not Fat Either*), and a chick-lit series called *Queen of Babble*, about a young woman who talks too much, a personality trait with which Meg is completely unfamiliar

Meg divides her time between New York City, Key West, and Indiana with a primary cat (one-eyed Henrietta), various back-up cats, and her husband. Visit her website at www.megcabot.com.

Eoin Colfer is the author of the bestselling *Artemis Fowl* and the other books in the series: *The Arctic Incident, The Eternity Code, The Opal Deception* and *The Lost Colony* – as well as several separate novels including *The Wish List* and *The Supernaturalist*. His latest series is the detective adventure *Half Moon Investigations*. A former schoolteacher, Eoin lives in Wexford, Ireland.

Joe Craig is the author of the award-winning *Jimmy Coates* series. Before becoming a novelist he studied Philosophy at Cambridge University then worked as a songwriter and jazz musician. When not writing, he visits schools, invents snacks, plays football and cricket, reads, watches movies and keeps in touch with readers via his website, www.joecraig.co.uk

Annie Dalton has written many books, including the award-winning *The After Dark Princess* and the Carnegie Medal shortlisted *The Real Tilly Beany*. She is the author of the hugely successful *Agent Angels* series, which has been sold to several countries and optioned as a film by Disney. Annie lives in Norfolk, in a cottage with a castle at the bottom of the garden (well, allegedly. You can't actually see it for the trees). She has three children and two grandchildren.

Terry Denton's books include *Gasp!*, *Duck for Cover* and *Sucked In!*. In 1986 *Felix and Alexander* was named a Children's Book Council of Australia Book of the Year Award winner, and since then he has illustrated more than thirty books, ten of which he has also written. His most recent books include *The Bad Book* (with Andy Griffiths).

Chris d'Lacey has written a wide variety of books for children of all ages, but is best known for his series of dragon titles, the latest of which is *The Fire Eternal*. He is a regular visitor to schools, libraries and book festivals. For more information, check out his personal website: www.icefire.co.uk

Helen Dunmore is a novelist, children's writer and poet. She won the inaugural Orange Prize for Fiction for her novel *A Spell of Winter*. The second volume in her *Ingo* series of novels for children, *The Tide Knot*, was published in 2006, and shortlisted for The Nestlé Children's Prize. Helen Dunmore is a Fellow of The Royal Society of Literature.

Jackie French is a full-time writer, who lives in New South Wales, Australia. Her award-winning books for children include *Hitler's Daughter* and her lovely picture book *Diary of a Wombat*. She has published over one hundred and fifteen books, of which the latest to be published in the UK is *Slave Girl*.

Maeve Friel is the author of the popular *Witch-in-Training* series as well as books for younger children including *Felicity Floss: Tooth Fairy* and *Felix on the Move*. She was born in Derry, Northern Ireland but now divides her time between Dublin and a small village in Southern Spain.

Neil Gaiman has spent his adult life making things up and writing them down. He lives more in America than he does anywhere else. He has written books like *Neverwhere* and *Stardust* and films like *MirrorMask* and children's books like *Coraline*. He has a blog over at www.neilgaiman.com, and a website about his childrens books at www.mousecircus.com. He's won more than his fair share of literary awards, was voted twenty-first equal on a recent magazine poll of Great British Authors, and has no idea where he put his keys.

Morris Gleitzman has been a frozen-chicken thawer, sugar-mill rolling-stock unhooker, fashion-industry trainee, department-store Santa, TV producer, newspaper columnist and screenwriter. Then he had a wonderful experience. He wrote a novel for young people. Now he's one of Australia's most popular children's authors. His books include *Boy Overboard*, *Worm Story* and *Once*.

Andy Griffiths is the author of *The Day My Bum Went Psycho*, *Zombi Bums from Uranus* and *Bumageddon: The Final Pongflict*, as well as the JUST series, and *The Bad Book* (with Terry Denton). Andy divides his time between bum-fighting and working on the final book in the BUM Trilogy. You can find out more about Andy and his stupid books at www.andygriffiths.com.au

Tony Hart undertook formal art training at Maidstone Art College, then struggled as a freelance artist, often painting murals on restaurant walls in return for free meals. His luck changed when, in 1952, he met a TV producer at a party and was invited to come for an interview. After demonstrating his skill by drawing a fish on a BBC paper napkin – which had been provided with his coffee – he was engaged as the resident artist on the BBC Children's TV programme *Saturday Special*. Tony's programmes went on to win a multitude of international awards, including a BAFTA – and in the meantime he created the original design for the Blue Peter badge. *Hartbeat* often attracted some five and a half million viewers, and Tony's mailbag varied between 6,000 and 8,000 per week, needing a large team of senior citizens to deal with it.

Anthony Horowitz is a hugely popular author of books for young readers. He has just begun a major new series of supernatural thrillers, beginning with *Raven's Gate*, but he is best known for the Alex Rider books, which have sold eight million copies worldwide. *Stormbreaker*, a major movie based on the first Alex Rider novel, was released in 2006.

Brian Jacques was born and brought up in Liverpool, became a merchant seaman at the age of fifteen and travelled the world. His *Redwall* books have sold over two million copies worldwide and have been translated into several different languages. The latest books in the *Redwall* series are *Triss*, *Loamhedge* and *Rakkety Tam*.

Oliver Jeffers is a painter, illustrator and writer. His picture books for children are *How to Catch a Star*, *Lost and Found* (which won the Gold Award at the Nestlé Children's Book Prize in 2005) and *The Incredible Book Eating Boy*. His website is www.oliverjeffers.com

Derek Landy began his career as a scriptwriter, creating the screenplays for a zombie movie and a murderous thriller in which everybody dies. His debut children's novel, *Skulduggery Pleasant*, was published in 2007. As a black belt in Kenpo Karate, Derek has taught countless children how to defend themselves, in the hopes of building his own private munchkin army. He firmly believes that they await his call to strike against his enemies (he doesn't actually *have* any enemies, but he's assuming they'll show up, sooner or later).

Katherine Langrish grew up in Yorkshire. When she was ten, she wrote a new 'Narnia' story in an old blue notebook and has never stopped writing since. She is the author of the fantasy series *Troll Fell*, *Troll Mill* and *Troll Blood*, based on Scandinavian folklore and Viking legends. While researching the latest book she learned how to sail a reconstructed Viking Age ship on a Danish fjord. Katherine has lived in France and the USA, but she now lives in Oxfordshire and enjoys her life as a full time author.

David Mackintosh is an Australian illustrator now living in London, best known for his picture books with Gillian Rubinstein, including *Sharon, Keep Your Hair On*.

Margaret Mahy is from New Zealand and she became the first writer outside the UK to win the Carnegie Medal — for *The Haunting* — winning the same award two years later for *The Changeover*. Her other novels include *Memory*, *Twenty-Four Hours*, *Riddle of the Frozen Phantom* and her most recent, *Alchemy*. In 2006 she won the Hans Christian Andersen Award, in recognition of a lasting contribution to children's literature.

Garth Nix has worked as a bookseller, book sales representative, publicist, editor, marketing consultant and, most recently, as a literary agent. He currently writes full time and his books are published around the world and are widely translated. They include the bestselling *Sabriel*, *Lirael* and *Abhorsen*, and his Keys to the Kingdom series.

Jamie Oliver started cooking at his parents' pub, The Cricketers, at the age of eight. He is now one of the world's best known chefs and celebrities. He also started Cheeky Chops, a charity which provides training and mentoring for disadvantaged young people — allowing them to follow their dreams and become chefs. More recently he has fronted a high-profile campaign for healthier lunches in schools.

Louise Rennison lives in Brighton, a place that she likes to think of as the San Francisco of the South Coast. Which is sad as it is nothing like San Francisco, being mainly pebbles and large people in tiny swimming knickers who have gone bright red in the sun. Although she lives in Brighton in reality, in her mind she lives somewhere exotic with a manservant called Juan. This is because she lost her mind after *Angus, Thongs and Full-Frontal Snogging*, the first book in her hilarious series, *The Confessions of Georgia Nicolson*, catapulted her into the spotlight of fame.

Darren Shan wrote twelve books about vampires, and is now writing The Demonata – ten books about demons. Despite his grisly subject matter, he is relatively harmless. Unless there is a full moon.

Jonathan Stroud is the author of the bestselling Bartimaeus Trilogy, comprising *The Amulet of Samarkand*, *The Golem's Eye* and *Ptolemy's Gate*. His other novels are *The Last Siege*, *The Leap* and *Buried Fire*. He lives in Hertfordshire, where he is currently hard at work scribbling in a darkened room.

Eleanor Updale's *Montmorency* series has won international prizes, including the Blue Peter "Book I couldn't put down" award, and Best Book

About War Child

War Child was set up in 1993 by two journalists who were working in the war in the Balkans region of Europe. They saw many terrible things, and saw how many, many children were massively affected by the war — from being injured, losing parents or starving, to not being able to get to school or to play.

The war did a very good job of taking away the normal things a child would do, and War Child wanted to change that.

Since then, War Child has worked with millions of children and their families affected by war all over the world. Sadly we've been very busy, but we hope that we've helped many children get back to doing those things that all kids everywhere want to do. We've worked in places like Colombia and Guatemala, East Timor, Kosovo and Rwanda. Currently, War Child works in the Democratic Republic of Congo, Iraq and Afghanistan: and we *still* work in Bosnia, with children who are still affected by a conflict that ended over a decade ago.

We work with children who have experienced things no child should ever have to go through. In Congo, War Child works to help former child soldiers reunite with their families and communities, and helps some of the older ones – who now have children themselves – start small businesses to look after their families.

In Afghanistan, War Child works with boys and girls who have become involved with criminal gangs, or have ended up in prisons because of family disputes. War Child has found that many of these children have ended up in adult prisons – extremely dangerous places for young people. War Child helped to set up child-only detention centres where these children can rehabilitate properly, away from the fear of grown-up criminals.

In Iraq, War Child is working with some of the many children who have ended up living and working on the street – because their families are so poor, or because their father was killed or injured in the war. Many of these children sell goods on the street, some sell drugs and guns. These streets of Iraqi cities are especially dangerous for children. For these children War Child has set up Drop-In Centres, where they might be able to learn trades, or learn to read and write.

In 2003 War Child published its first book of stories for children. Called *Kids Night In,* the book raised loads of money for our work. We hope *Midnight Feast* will do the same – so thank you for buying it!

If you'd like to read more about our work, why not visit our website www.warchildmusic.com. If you like music, you can download exclusive tracks there too – every download raises money for War Child's work, so you can help us while you check out the latest tunes!

(Make sure a parent or guardian knows you are doing this – you'll need their permission to pay for the tracks you download)

IRAQ KENNETH O'HALLORAN

HOW WAR CHILD CHANGES LIVES

Faisal Sa'ad is fifteen. He sells bananas on the streets of Basra, Iraq. This is his story.

I am a banana seller. I sell bananas on the streets. My father died when I was very young. I live with my mother, my three older brothers and my sister. My brothers work and our uncle helps us with money but it is hard — so I have to work. I hate working on the street but I have to help look after my family. It is dangerous, dirty and exhausting.

The streets are full of people trying to get children to do awful things, like sell drugs, or move guns around the city. The streets are violent: when there is fighting no one is safe at all. Sometimes after a battle, there are bombs left in the road. The buildings are crumbling and very dangerous — but the younger kids like to play in them, like climbing frames, because there is nowhere else to play...

When my brothers heard about War Child's Drop-In Centre, they insisted I should come here and stay off the street. My brothers know that this is a safe place, and somewhere I will learn, so I can definitely get a proper job when I am a bit older.

Before I started coming here, I worked from six in the morning until it got dark. Now I stay at the Centre all morning until it shuts at one and learn about car mechanics. I go home for lunch and then although I still have to go to work, at least when I'm at the centre I am safe and learning.

We get fed breakfast here at the centre but the most important thing is the education. Food is possible to find, but if you lost your education you may never have the chance to learn again.

By buying *Midnight Feast*, you are helping War Child's work with children like Faisal. If you'd like to do even more to help why not log on to www.warchildmusic.com and download some cool music? We've got everything on there from Sugababes to Gorillaz, from Feeder to the Arctic Monkeys!

Or why not set up your own event in your school or community…?

(Make sure a parent or guardian knows you are doing this — you'll need their permission to pay for the tracks you download)

HOW YOU CAN HELP!

You can help War Child yourself in loads of different, brilliant and easy ways!

Sponsored events — like a sponsored swim, but what about a sponsored read, or a sponsored silence!?! — are great because they can get loads of people involved.

Mufti days are great because you get to wear what you want to wear to school...

...so why not set up a fashion show, a disco or a karaoke event on the day?

Why not charge your families to attend the school play?

School competitions are great – you could organise a *Mastermind* event, a five-a-side tournament or a netball marathon – because they get everyone excited.

Really simple things can generate a lot of coverage – why not make a big peace sign in your school field? You could charge everyone a pound to participate, and you'll be guaranteed to get the local newspaper there to take a photo of it...!

You could even raise money by doing jobs around your community – dog walking, car washing – and give out leaflets about War Child at the same time.

You could even write to your local MP and ask him or her what they are doing about children in war zones – perhaps they might come into your school and do a *Question Time* event?

You can find loads of different ideas on our website www.warchildmusic.com – you could even download some music for your disco!!!

(Make sure a parent or guardian knows you are doing this – you'll need their permission to pay for the tracks you download)

IRAQ KENNETH O'HALLORAN

About No Strings

No Strings International is a charity that uses puppets to teach life-saving messages to children and their families who live in the developing world. Many children in other parts of the world cannot read and write or even go to school, so using puppets is a really good way of teaching them in a fun and interesting way.

No Strings is running an important project in Afghanistan. Afghanistan has a long history of war, and as a result there are nearly eight million landmines in the country. A landmine is a small unexploded bomb buried under the ground. If a person steps on one it can be very dangerous as it can seriously injure or even kill them. No Strings has created an educational puppet film, *ChucheQhalin*, which teaches children where landmines are most likely to be lurking, and how to avoid them. It uses characters based on traditional Afghan stories, and is told in their own languages. The main characters are Chuchi, a little boy made of carpet, and his camel, Jaladul, who have lots of adventures together. Thousands of children have already seen the film thanks to their Afghan partner OMAR. They have their own TV station, and they also take it into schools on a mobile media motorbike. This eRanger motorbike is very special as it turns into a cinema so can show the film to children who live in the most far-away places.

CHUCHI

One of the children who has seen the film is called Masaud and is 12 years old. Masaud was born and lives in Kabul, the capital city of Afghanistan. This is his story.

"My name is Masaud, and I am 12. In my country, children love to fly kites. It's a big national sport. For me though, it's probably not something I will be able to do again. Two years ago in October 2004, as I was jumping up to catch my kite, I stepped on an unseen landmine buried in the road. The explosion took off my left leg, from just below the hip. It happened right in the centre of Kabul, just 100  metres from the Presidential Palace. It shows that there are landmines everywhere in Afghanistan. My other leg was injured. I still have to wear bandages but it's OK. No-one is safe from landmines in our country, especially children. Luckily, none of my four brothers or six sisters have been injured, but I know many children who have.

"After my accident, I had to spend a whole year in hospital. I think the happiest day of my life was when they gave me my artificial leg. It means that I can walk the same as other children, with just a slight limp. At school, I'm in the 8th class. I love school. I like reading and writing, and I love football even though now I can only watch it. I also love watching TV, although I don't like action movies. I like normal, Afghan TV.

"When I saw the No Strings Chuchi film about landmines, the first thing I thought was that I wish I'd seen it two years ago, before my accident. It would be wonderful if all the children in Afghanistan could see it. I think its message is very clear and easy to understand. It's also fun to watch. Now that I've seen it, I know not to touch things as they may be dangerous, and I know how to look out for danger signs. I've also learned to listen to what people are saying all the time."

And it doesn't stop there. No Strings is developing the use of the same puppets in Afghanistan to teach about drug and health issues. They are also creating puppet films with new characters for Sri Lanka and Indonesia to teach about natural disasters such as tsunami and earthquakes, and they hope to teach about HIV/AIDS in Africa soon too. By buying this book you will be helping change children's lives all over the world. Thank you.

If you would like more information about No Strings please visit www.nostrings.org.uk